REDEMPTION

A SOULMATES DARK SECRETS DARK MAFIA ROMANCE

STRUCK IN LOVE
BOOK FIVE

CHIQUITA DENNIE

304 PUBLISHING COMPANY

LATEST RELEASES FROM CHIQUITA DENNIE

Latest Releases from Chiquita Dennie
The Early Years-A Prequel Short Story
Antonio and Sabrina: Struck in Love 1, 2, 3, 4, 5
Heart of Stone, Book 1 (Emery & Jackson)
Heart Of Stone Book 1.5 Emery &Jackson A Valentine's Day Short
Janice and Carlo: Captivated By His Love
Heart of Stone, Book 2 (Jordan and Damon)
Temptation
Heart of Stone, Book 3 (Angela and Brent)
Cocky Catcher
Bossy Billionaire
Bottoms Up Heart of Stone, Book 3.5 (Jessica and Joseph Short
Love Shorts: A Collection of Short Stories
Joaquin Fuertes (The Fuertes Cartel Book 1)
Exposed (Salvation Society Novel)
Joaquin Fuertes (The Fuertes Cartel Book 2)
Refuel (A Driven World Novel)
Pressure (A Driven World Novel)

LATEST RELEASES FROM CHIQUITA DENNIE

Until Serena (HEA World Novel)
Antonio and Sabrina: Struck in Love 5
Heart of Stone, Book 4 (Jessica and Joseph)
She's All I Need
Red Light District (A Fantasy Romance Short)
Something Gaine(Romantic Comedy)
Upcoming Releases (2022/2023):
Aydin-TN Security Book 1
Dare To Love
The Carrington Cartel Book 1
Something Earned (A Romantic Comedy)
The Carrington Cartel Book 2

DISCLAIMER

This work of fiction contains strong language and explicit sexual content and is only intended for mature readers. This story may contain unconventional situations, language, and sexual encounters that may offend some readers. If you're looking for sweet, fluffy romance, I would recommend another book. This book is for mature readers (18+).

ACKNOWLEDGMENTS

I want to thank, first and foremost, God for giving me the strength to not give up and focus on not only my health and mental roadblocks, but also giving me the gift of storytelling. The most important woman in my life and biggest support system, my mom, Rhonda Dennie, my brother Brent Dennie, JD, Chris, and the entire family, without you and the family behind me none of this would be possible. Also, I would like to send a shout out to Elaine, Mercedes, and Kinney for helping me along the way in this author world.

AUTHOR INSPIRATION

"*Never allow anyone to steal your joy. It doesn't matter how many times someone says you can't do something. Invest in yourself—even if it's just writing down what your goals and plans are. Starting small can lead to bigger things.*"

—Chiquita Dennie

INTRODUCTION

Are you signed up for my newsletter?

Join today and find out all the latest in new releases, contests, giveaways, sneak peeks and more.

www.chiquitadennie.com

DISCLAIMER

This work of fiction contains strong language and explicit sexual content and is only intended for mature readers. This story may contain unconventional situations, language, and sexual encounters that may offend some readers. If you're looking for sweet, fluffy romance, I would recommend another book. This book is for mature readers (18+).

SYNOPSIS

They say you can never go back home again…

Antonio:

I thought that getting out of prison would be a dream come true.

Prison was supposed to be the hard part after all.

When I'm reunited with my family, though, I realize that the hard work has only just begun.

Sabrina:

Having Antonio back with us was supposed to be a happy day.

Instead, it only seems to have caused more problems.

Our son is acting out, Antonio is back at the helm of the cartel and dealing with all of those problems, and now old secrets are coming to life and threatening to destroy all of us.

After all these two have endured together, will the family be able to withstand another attack?

The courthouse seemed to get smaller and smaller as the prosecutor presented evidence of Queen's murder. I tried my best to stay focused and not show any kind of facial expression that would let everyone know how scared and worried about my husband I was.

He was the most known criminal in New York City, and I wished we would have stayed in Italy and raised our children. The De Luca name came with a lot of privilege; at the same time, it was a curse that so often left families broken—children without their fathers, and wives without their husbands.

I stared as the reporters continued to write every word the prosecutor said, making it seem like Queen was this honorable woman who provided for the community and worked to create communication and a new partnership between Italy and America. I gritted my teeth at the notion of her being some kind of Mother Theresa.

The moment she came for my husband and children, I didn't have any regrets about what happened to her, and if

I had the chance, I wish Antonio would have let me handle her, so we wouldn't be in this predicament now.

The prosecutor removed the second photo of Queen's dismembered remains. I still had no idea how they'd traced everything back to Antonio, but there we were, watching the closing arguments, and the judge giving the final verdict. I asked our attorney, Felicia Marsh, what chances we had of getting off, and she looked soberly at me and told me to prepare my children. In that moment, I was close to breaking down because I'd been with this man for over 15 years, and now it came down to a judge to decide whether my husband was guilty or not.

My mother covered my hand with hers as the prosecutor rested his case. The long breath I held finally released as he named everything that the De Luca Cartel was into, from racketeering and gun sales to drugs, kidnappings, and bribery. I knew some people wondered if I knew that my husband was into all those things at the beginning, would I still have married him. The honest answer was yes. Antonio De Luca was the love of my life, and the man people saw when he was away from his family was not the same man he showed to us. I understood why he had to be that way; it was because after the death of his father, the tension between the families had only grown wider.

"Sabrina, maybe you should take a break and get some air," Mom whispered.

I shook my head. "I cannot leave him," I replied, wiping away the tear that was starting to fall down my face.

"Honey, he knows you love him," Mom stated.

But I wasn't going to walk away—no matter what happened.

"Ladies and gentlemen, we have come to the end of

these court proceedings, and I've heard from defense attorneys and prosecutors," Judge Ramiro explained.

I felt my body tense at every word he said. Antonio stared straight ahead, as though it wouldn't matter either way. Sofia and Joaquin had wanted to be here, too, but I told them not to come; it would have only caused even more drama with the media.

"All rise," the bailiff announced.

"Mr. De Luca, I hereby—" The judge was interrupted as the doors opened, and Gael walked inside, holding an envelope. Gael walked over to his lawyer, as the judge slammed his gavel down.

"This is my courtroom; I will not allow interruptions," Judge Ramiro stated.

Gael whispered something to Felicia and slid her the envelope. Antonio leaned over and looked at the contents of the envelope.

His lawyer stood up. "Sorry, Your Honor. We have new evidence," Felicia Marsh stated, causing the entire room to blow up in excitement.

"Your Honor, we don't have time for the De Luca cartel to bring up last-minute evidence," District Attorney Grady Fletcher said.

"Bring the envelope to me, and we'll call for a five-minute recess," Judge Ramiro said.

Felicia lifted the contents of the envelope and headed toward the judge's bench. Grady and Felicia argued back and forth in front of the judge. Gael came to sit next to me.

"What was that?" I asked Gael.

"Joaquin got evidence to show that Antonio wasn't there when Queen was killed," Gael explained.

"What evidence?"

"He was in a meeting," Gael told me.

"What type of meeting?"

"Antonio was meeting with the other bosses," Gael mentioned, and my heart sank because more than likely, something illegal had happened at the meeting that could come back to hurt Antonio.

"Try not to worry; Felicia's good," Gael said, and I couldn't argue with him about that, but there were circumstances that continued to haunt our family almost 15 years later.

The judge came back out of his chambers, along with the lawyers. "With this new evidence, I will need more time before making a final decision," the judge said.

"Your Honor, I would like to move for dismissal of all charges," Felicia stated.

"Your client will stay in custody until I investigate further," Judge Ramiro said, and Antonio gave him a harsh glare as the courtroom erupted into chaos again.

"Your Honor, my client isn't a flight risk; he is a business owner, and he has four children in school," Felicia explained, and I thought of having to continue to tell our kids the same lie, that their father was away on business.

"I'll make my decision soon," Judge Ramiro said, slamming his gavel down and adjourning.

I tried to talk to Antonio, but the guards removed him from the courtroom first. He was shackled around the waist, legs and hands; he looked like he'd lost a little weight.

Carlo and Gael escorted me out of the courtroom as Felicia approached us out front. "Gael, I need to know everything, so I can help get Antonio out of jail," Felicia said, removing her business card out of her pocket.

"When can I see Antonio?" I asked.

"I'm sorry, Sabrina; Antonio asked to not see anyone except Carlo," Felicia mentioned, and I gasped in shock. For the last two months, it had been the same thing:

Antonio not letting me see him, with only one phone call a week.

"He's decided to ignore my requests?" I asked, getting more agitated with his attitude towards me. At 38, I wasn't the same woman he'd met at Ryde all those years ago and ignoring me would only make me even more pissed off.

"Felicia, tell him either I see him this weekend, or divorce papers will be delivered," I spat, walked off to my car, where Salvatore was waiting in the driver's seat. I slid inside, Carlo jumped into the passenger seat, and Gael strolled to his jeep behind us. We pulled out into traffic.

* * *

THIRTY MINUTES LATER, I arrived home and heard the kids playing, oblivious to where their father was. Carlo stepped inside, talking on his phone—more than likely, to Antonio's lawyer. I went to the living room and noticed Isabella playing with Luca and Jonathan.

"Where's AJ?" I questioned, interrupting their video game.

"Hi, Mommy!" Isabella said and ran over, hugging me around the waist.

I bent down and hugged Isabella, pressing a kiss against her cheek. My baby girl looked just like her father. She smiled and showed off her beautiful smile, and I tugged on the long pigtails I'd styled earlier that morning.

Every day, I thanked God for blessing me with amazing kids who hadn't been scared off by the environment that the De Luca Cartel brought to the family. The lie we decided to tell the kids was that their father was out of the country on business because since his father was killed, he'd taken on a bigger role in the family. The only problem was that AJ, our oldest son, knew what his father did for a living, and since Antonio had been gone, he was starting to act out a little.

"Hi, Mom!" Jonathan and Luca said as Emilia came into the living room.

Emilia was an older woman who Janice recommended from her nanny service. They specialized in staffing for high-profile families. She was in her early 50s, a widower, and had two kids that had families of their own. I'd hired her two years ago to help around the house after Luca arrived.

I still worked part-time at Washington Finance as CEO; I had brought on a president to work in a daily capacity since my father retired.

"Hi, Mrs. De Luca; I just finished making lunch for the kids. Are you joining them?" Emilia asked.

"Hi, Emilia; yes, I just need to talk with Carlo really quick," I said, watching Isabella run over to her brothers.

"Where's AJ?" Carlo asked, ending his call.

"He's in his room," Emilia answered.

I headed up the spiral stairs of the three-story stonewall Spanish-style mansion with Carlo behind me. The house was massive, and I'd told Antonio that we didn't need that much space, but he was adamant about his family being safe at all times. however, I was thinking of moving us out of the city and maybe homeschooling the kids again instead of keeping them in private school. Originally, I'd had to fight Antonio to even let me put them in private school. He'd wanted homeschooling, but I saw AJ constantly withdrawing while he was always stuck in the house and not around other kids his own age, plus having to take on the responsibility of his younger siblings.

"Janice said to call her when you get a chance," Carlo said, sliding his phone into his pocket.

"She wanted to know what to do about a contract; I'll call her later," I said, tapping on the door of AJ's room.

"Yeah!" AJ called out.

I pushed the door open. My firstborn was almost as tall as me at only 14 years old. He looked exactly like his father, and I knew that was trouble. Already, girls were calling the house, wanting to talk to him.

All the kids were spoiled, but Antonio took extra time with AJ and Isabella because he was the firstborn, and she was the only girl. He was soft with our daughter; she was the light of Antonio's life, and I knew he was missing her just as much as she was missing him. People would never expect to see the big bad gangster, sipping on tea and playing with dolls, but anything Isabella wanted, Antonio did. He wasn't this completely evil, soulless man, the way the press made him out to be.

"I see you cleaned your room, like I asked." I watched as he lay on his back with his video game in hand. I glanced at the floor, which was finally cleared of the clothes and shoes that had been piled up.

"Ma, not now," AJ said.

"You know better than to talk to your mother like that, AJ," Carlo said, walking toward AJ and ripping the game out of his hands.

"What the fuck?!" AJ shouted.

"Hey, watch your language. Your father may not be here, but I am," Carlo demanded, tossing the game in the trash.

I groaned, rubbing my temples and praying that things would get better once Antonio came home. AJ had been acting out since his father got locked up, and he blamed both of us.

"Whatever," he mumbled and tried to turn his back to us.

"AJ, come down to have lunch with us," I said.

"I'm not hungry," AJ said, burying his head in his pillow.

"What's your problem, AJ? Your mother is trying to be patient with you, but not me," Carlo explained.

"Nothing," AJ replied, and we both knew that was a lie.

"AJ, when your father comes home, what do you think he'll say?" I asked.

"He's not coming home. Don't lie to me like you do to the other kids," AJ argued, jumping out of bed and trying to walk out.

Carlo gripped him by his shirt and forced him against the door. "Look at me. Hey! Stop being disrespectful to your mother, or I'll put my foot up your ass," Carlo demanded.

I tried to get Carlo to release him. "It's okay, Carlo."

"No, it's not; don't let him act like a spoiled brat. That's his problem," Carlo said.

"Uncle Carlo, let me go," AJ said and tried to push Carlo's hand down.

"I will when you apologize to your mother," Carlo said.

"Sorry," AJ stated, rolling his eyes.

Carlo tapped him on the forehead with his finger. "A *real* apology, boy," Carlo said.

"I apologize, Mommy," AJ said.

Carlo released him, and AJ came over to give me a hug. He stood around 5'6" already. I thought he would be as tall as his father when he turned 18.

"I love you, baby." I kissed him on his forehead.

"Ma, stop; I'm not a baby," AJ said and tried to get out of my arms.

"You'll always be my baby," I teased, kissing him again.

"I know Dad's in jail; you don't have to hide the truth from me," AJ commented.

We walked out of his room and downstairs to the

kitchen, where we ate most of the time. I had a nice dining room, but the kids all came into the kitchen whenever I was cooking to hang out and eat.

"How do you know that?" I asked, no longer hiding it from him, since he was old enough to know the truth.

"Uncle Carlo was talking to him on the phone one time, and I overheard him," AJ explained as we walked into the kitchen. Emilia placed food in front of Luca and Jonathan.

Isabella ran toward AJ, and he picked her up in his arms. She was six, but the princess of the family. "AJ came to play with dolls with me," Isabella said.

"What did you cook, Emilia? Smells good," I stated, picked up Jonathan's fork, and took a bite of his pasta.

"AJ's favorite—smoked mozzarella pasta," Emilia told me, and I grabbed a plate for myself and started to pick at all the food on the stove.

"Uncle Carlo, are you staying to eat with us?" Isabella asked.

"No, princess; I need to get home to your cousins," Carlo responded, pinching her cheek.

I sat next to Jonathan, across from AJ and Isabella. Luca was sitting on top of the island, eating a bowl of pasta. My baby was the miracle we'd needed after the miscarriage; he'd helped us heal.

"Mommy, when is Daddy coming home?" Isabella inquired, taking a sip of her water.

"Soon, baby."

AJ and Carlo both glanced at me somberly.

"He works too hard," Isabella commented, and I nodded.

Emilia started to put the rest of the food away, and I motioned for her to take a seat. "I'll clean it up, Emilia; don't worry."

"Sabrina, call me later," Carlo muttered, treading out of the kitchen, and I waved goodbye.

"How about tonight, we watch a movie?" I asked them.

"Yay!" the three youngest yelled out in excitement.

AJ stole a piece of chicken off Jonathan's plate.

*L*ater in the evening, after we finished lunch and cleaned up around the house, I made a few calls and checked in with Felicia about Antonio. Then I took a shower. The kids were in the living room, getting the movie ready. When I stepped out with a towel around my hair, I picked up my cell to finally call Janice back.

"You *do* remember me," Janice said.

"Don't start, Janice." I dried my hair off, stepped out of the bathroom to grab my scarf, and found a pair of pants and Antonio's shirt to sleep in.

"Carlo told me AJ was acting up today," Janice said.

"He's hurting; that's all."

"You need me to talk with him?" Janice asked.

"Your idea of talking to your kids is yelling at them because they put stretch marks on your body," I responded.

"I don't yell. I just speak at a high volume," Janice commented, as I sat down at my vanity mirror to brush my hair.

"Mommy, it's ready!" Isabella yelled.

"Okay, baby." I said, stood up to slide my feet into my house shoes, and walked out of my room.

"Have you talked to him since court today?" Janice questioned.

I heard her kids arguing in the background. "What are my babies doing?" I asked.

"Getting on my nerves. I told them I'll send them to your house, or my parents to have a break," Janice said.

I laughed at her statement as AJ came out of the kitchen with a bowl of popcorn. "Leave them alone. Hopefully, he'll call me tonight."

"Did you tell Felicia to get your message across?" Janice asked.

"I did. I told her if he doesn't let me come see him, then we're getting a divorce," I mumbled into the phone. I sat next to Isabella on the couch, pulling a blanket across my legs.

"Good; keep me updated. Are you coming into the office?" Janice wondered.

"Probably. I need to make sure the kids are good first," I responded, then said goodnight and ended the call.

"What movie are we watching?" AJ asked.

"*Captain America.*" Jonathan said.

AJ groaned in annoyance. "We watched that movie a million times, man," AJ stated and tried to grab the remote from his brother.

"It's my turn to pick!" Jonathan yelled out.

"AJ, leave your brother alone," I said.

He stuck his tongue out at his brother, and I slapped the back of his head for being mean.

"What'd I do?" AJ asked.

"Leave your brother alone," I remarked again, and the movie started.

After a few minutes, my phone started ringing from an unknown number. "Hello," I answered.

"Bella," Antonio said.

I almost cried in front of the kids because we couldn't have him near us. I cleared my throat and eased away from Isabella to take the call in the other room. "Antonio."

"How are you, Bella?" Antonio questioned.

"I miss you."

I heard a sigh from the other end of the phone. "I miss you, too, baby. How are the kids?" Antonio inquired.

I went into the kitchen to grab a glass of water. "They miss you."

"I'll be home soon."

"How? the judge seems to have it out for you."

"It's all a part of the plan, baby."

"What plan? Tell me what's going on, Antonio." I turned around and saw AJ standing in the kitchen doorway. "I'll be back in there in a minute, AJ."

"Is that Dad?" he asked.

"AJ," I urged.

"Bella, it's all right. Let me talk to him for a second."

"Whose phone are you using?" I queried.

"Mine," Antonio responded, and I passed the phone to AJ. We sat together on the bench in the corner of the kitchen.

"When are you coming home?" AJ asked.

"AJ," I warned him.

"Soon, son. Are you helping your mom with your brothers and sister?" Antonio questioned.

AJ glanced up at me. He knew he hadn't been on his best behavior lately, but I let him get away with a lot of things because when I was kidnapped years ago and gave birth to AJ in Italy, it was just the two of us trying to survive and make it back home safely.

"Yeah, but I want you to come home," AJ said.

I pulled him into my arms.

"I know, son. But listen to your mom because Carlo told me you've been talking back to her," Antonio told him.

"I will," AJ muttered, passing the phone back to me. He had the same curly hair and dark brown skin tone as his father. When he grew up, I'd be ready to kill any girl that hurt my baby. He pressed a kiss to my forehead, like his father always did, and I smiled, watching as he walked out to go watch the movie.

"He's turning into a little Antonio De Luca," I said.

"I want him to be better than me," Antonio remarked.

"You're the best man in the world. AJ is lucky to have a father like you."

"What about you?" Antonio asked.

I grinned at his statement. "Let's be honest; the moment you met me in your club, I was hooked."

"We were both hooked," Antonio teased.

"I'm thinking of moving the kids," I announced.

"No. You're safe there," Antonio said.

"Antonio, we don't know how long this will last."

"I was trying to avoid going into detail, but they're after one of the bosses, and they want to use me," Antonio said.

"What do you mean?"

"The charges against me for killing Queen aren't high priority," Antonio mentioned.

"Are you saying they're using you to get to someone else?"

"I'll explain more later. I just want to see you," Antonio said.

"What are you talking about?"

"Turn your phone on Facetime, so we can see each other," Antonio explained.

I stood up, shook my head, and went to check on the kids in the living room. "You're crazy; I'm not doing that."

"Why not? It's only me in here," Antonio grunted.

"No, not about to do that with the kids still awake."

"Bella," Antonio called me by nickname.

"I promise when you get home, I'll give you a real show on camera," I teased and sat on the couch next to a sleeping Isabella.

"Felicia should have some news for you tomorrow," Antonio mentioned.

I rubbed the top of Isabella's hair as Jonathan and AJ stared at the TV. Both Luca and Isabella were knocked out and snoring. "Okay, I'll try and meet with her tomorrow."

"I'll be thinking about you in my dreams tonight," Antonio stated.

I closed my eyes and thought of the last time we made love without any interruptions. It was the night before he was arrested. "I love you."

"I love you, too, Sabrina," Antonio replied, and I listened to his breathing on the other line before he hung up.

I lifted Isabella up and tapped AJ to grab Luca, so we could put them to bed.

"Ma, did you ever think to leave the cartel?" AJ asked.

"To be honest, AJ, you never really leave the cartel," I said, and we headed upstairs and put them both to bed. I told him to not stay up too late with his brother.

* * *

THE NEXT MORNING, I poured a cup of coffee as the kids ran around the kitchen, gathering their things for school. Emilia was there to take care of Luca, while I dropped the other kids off at school. Salvatore was there, too, along with Sonny, while Carlo was still handling things with Felicia.

"AJ, hurry up with your breakfast." I checked the time on my watch and noticed that I had an hour to drop them off and get to work.

"Mommy, are you going to work?" Isabella asked, eating some of her cereal.

"I am for a few hours, and you're going to school," I responded, sipping on my coffee and lifting a piece of toast off Jonathan's plate.

"Ma, stop eating my food," Jonathan said, pulling his plate closer to himself.

"You know, *my* money paid for that food, right?" I sassed, pouting.

"You mean yours and *Dad's* money. Share responsibilities," Jonathan joked.

I narrowed my eyes in hard slits at him. "Smart-ass," I said.

The doorbell rang. AJ jumped up to answer it, as I continued to talk with the kids. A few minutes later, Sonny walked inside.

"Sonny!" Luca screamed in excitement, trying to get down to hug him.

"Sonny, you didn't have to come today," I said. "I know you have a lot of work today." I let Enzo get down and run over, then Isabella tried to feed him her cereal.

Our family was really close with Antonio's men, ever since I gave birth to AJ all those years ago. It was Sonny who found us and brought us back to America.

"Hey, ladybug," Sonny stated, picking up Isabella to press a kiss on her cheek.

"I'm almost ready," I said, pouring out of the rest of my coffee as Emilia took the rest of the plates and discarded the food. "Emilia, I'll probably be late tonight.

Can you start dinner for me?" I asked, passing Jonathan his jacket.

"Yes, Mrs. De Luca," Emilia replied.

"Please, call me Sabrina."

"Of course, Sabrina." Emilia stated.

All the kids formed a line and started to walk out of the kitchen.

Sonny held the door open, while still carrying Isabella. "Salvatore is taking the kids to school, and I'm dropping you off," Sonny said. He put Isabella down, and she ran outside to the limo.

"Isabella, stop running," I called after her, then said to Sonny, "I still need to meet with Felicia."

"Did you call her yet?" Sonny opened the door of the Hummer.

"I left a message with her assistant, saying that I want to talk with her today."

"I have one meeting with Carlo, but I can run you over." Sonny started the car up as Salvatore drove off with the kids in front of us, and we went in the opposite direction.

"*D*id Antonio tell you how they arrested him?" I asked Sonny.

"He said you were home sleeping." Sonny pulled up to the red light.

* * *

Two Months Earlier

It was midnight on a Saturday. After watching movies with the kids for our weekly family night, Antonio went into his office to do some work on the club business.

"Daddy, I want to watch another movie," Isabella said, and everybody groaned in annoyance.

"Sweetheart, we've watched two of your movies. It's time for bed," Antonio sternly told her, and Isabella pouted with her lip poked out.

"She's so spoiled." AJ laughed at his sister.

I threw the pillow at him. "Time for bed. AJ, take your sister and brother," I said and picked up the pizza boxes and popcorn bowl. The cleaning service would have to come in on Monday to do a cleaning of the entire place.

Jonathan jumped up and helped AJ with Enzo, as Isabella stomped away. I walked into the kitchen and tossed the boxes away, then felt a pair of strong hands around my waist.

"I need to finish up some work in my office, and then I'll be up to bed," Antonio said.

"Okay. Don't be long," I said.

He bit the side of my neck, and I squealed in excitement. Our jobs always kept us both busy; this time of the year, I worked longer hours to help people who wanted to invest after tax season. Plus, it was hard to find alone time with our kids and families demanding our time. He smacked my ass, and I kissed him on the lips before he walked off.

An hour later, we were rolling around in bed together.

"Shit," Antonio grunted as I held onto his muscular chest and twisted my hips, while he hammered me from underneath.

"Fuck! Tony... yes!"

His hands seized my waist steadily as I dropped my head and scooted my ass up to fuck only his tip.

"Sabrina... wait, baby..." Antonio said.

I nibbled on his ear. I loved taking him to the edge. I continued to lick and moved down to circle his nipples with my tongue. "Who do you belong to?" I demanded, staring into his ocean blue eyes.

"Ah... fuck, Bella." Antonio's voice trembled, straining for relief. He thrust upward, taking control and turning me onto my back as he came with force.

"I knew you wouldn't last," I joked.

He bent down and captured my lips. "Shut up; that's not

funny, Bella." Antonio rested his heavy body against my chest, and we both fell into a deep sleep.

* * *

THIRTY MINUTES INTO OUR SLEEP, *I heard a loud banging at the front door that startled me out of my dreams. Antonio was snoring. I nudged him on the shoulder.*

Bang! Bang!

"Tony, wake up."

"Baby, I'm tired," Antonio muttered.

"No, I hear something." I smacked him lightly on the back of the head.

"Sabrina, what the fuck—"

Bang! Bang!

Antonio leaned over me and checked the time on the nightstand clock. He saw it read 2 AM. He jumped out of bed naked and grabbed his pajama pants and robe. I started to follow, but he held his hand up. "Stay here," he said, peeking out the window that faced the side street.

"What do you see?" I asked.

"DEA vans," he said.

"what?!" I yelled and charged over to the window. I tried to look, but he pushed me back.

"Put on some clothes and call Carlo," Antonio said and walked out of the bedroom.

I grabbed my robe and his t-shirt from earlier in the day and put them on. I stepped out of the room and noticed that AJ had awakened.

"Ma, what's going on?"

"Nothing. Go back to bed," I replied and walked down the stairs.

Antonio opened the door, and two DEA agents busted

through, holding a piece of paper. "Can I help you?" Antonio questioned.

"We have a warrant for your arrest and to search the premises," a tall, athletic man with a low-cut fade replied.

The guy standing next to him was shorter and stockier, with a toothpick in his mouth, bushy eyebrows, and a small scar along his jawline. "De Luca, we meet again," he said as I approached Antonio and stood next to him.

"Go back upstairs," Antonio said to me, and I shook my head.

The taller guy stared at me. "I take it this is the famous Mrs. De Luca. You don't remember me, but a friend of mine told me about you."

"I don't know who you or your friend are," I spat.

"DEA Agent James Roberts," he introduced himself. He pulled a business card from his wallet and passed it toward me.

Antonio ripped it up. "I don't give a shit who you are," he said through gritted teeth.

James grinned at me. "You sure you don't remember Derrick? He told me you went out on a date together and somehow, he ended up going missing."

I hadn't thought about Derrick in so long; it was like a faded memory. What happened to him was his own fault for trying to find evidence on Antonio.

Antonio tried to charge toward James.

I grabbed his arm. "Antonio, stop."

"Listen to your wife, Antonio, or we'll add interfering with a federal case to the list," James told him, getting in Antonio's face. They were both the same height, so I knew a fight was bound to happen—unless I took control of the scene.

"Baby, listen to me. Call your lawyer and let them do what they want. We have nothing to hide," I said.

"Your wife is very beautiful, Mr. De Luca. I'd hate to see her crying over you getting hurt," James announced.

"Mom!" AJ called out, and I turned my head to see the men tossing his clothes and shoes around.

"Go to your room and get your brothers and sisters," I said.

"Sabrina, go with the kids while I call Felicia," Antonio mentioned.

"I'm not leaving you alone with them," I argued.

James smirked and walked around us to head into the living room. "Oh, Mrs. De Luca? We have some of our friends checking out your business, as well." James stated.

"My company has nothing to do with my husband."

"I disagree; he has investments with your company. More than likely, he's using it to launder his dirty money." James informed me.

I had to shove Antonio back from trying to hit James in the face.

"You're so violent, Mr. De Luca; I think you should work on your feelings. I mean, I know you've gone to therapy in the past."

James's partner chuckled at his statement.

"Just do your job and get out of here," I spat.

A car pulled up, and we could hear arguing outside. Carlo, Janice, and Felicia were trying to come inside.

"Let them through!" I shouted, and the other agents looked at James for confirmation.

"What is going on here, Agent Roberts?" Felicia asked.

"Felicia, I thought you had better taste than taking on clients like Antonio De Luca here," James said.

"Who the fuck—"Antonio started to say.

"James, I suggest you and Harry finish, and if you're going to take my client to jail, then do it," Felicia announced.

"Jail! He can't do that!" I shouted.

Antonio pulled me into his arms, and I hugged him tight. "Shush... I'll be fine," Antonio said.

"What are they looking for?" Janice asked.

Felicia read the warrant and tossed it into her purse. "He's *being arrested on suspicion of the murder of Camilla Queen and former DEA Agent Derrick. Plus, tax fraud." She massaged her temples.*

"We've never had tax problems in our life," I said.

"Felicia, tell your client it's best to keep quiet because anything he says can and will be used against him," James grinned.

"I wouldn't be so cocky," Janice whispered.

"Oh, so this is Janice Russo. Your file came across my desk, and I think my people wanted to talk to you about Camilla's death, as well," James said.

"I don't know what you're talking about," Janice responded.

"Do your job but don't talk to my wife," Carlo commented.

*A*gent Roberts slid his hands into his pockets and motioned for his men to arrest Antonio. I wanted to kill all of them, but I thought about my kids and family. I walked to Antonio as the officer put the handcuffs on. He grunted from the tightness.

I stood on my tiptoes, pecked his lips, and lifted my arms around his neck. "I'll call my parents to watch the kids and come down to bail you out."

"That's not going to happen, Mrs. De Luca."

"Why not?"

"You want to explain it, Felicia?"

"Sabrina, it's a federal case. Let me handle things, please," Felicia informed me.

My bottom lip trembled, and tears welled in my eyes. "Oh, my God."

Antonio tried to bury his head in my chest, and they pulled him away. "Get the fuck off me!" Antonio shouted.

"Mommy!" I heard the cries of all my younger kids, and I rushed off upstairs to see what was happening.

* * *

I EXPLAINED the entire night to Sonny—except for our lovemaking. Weirdly enough, I thought of Sonny like a big brother. But he was part of Antonio's crew and over time, we had become friends.

"I remember Carlo calling me the next day about what was going on," Sonny responded, turning at the light and pulling up to the front of my office building.

"Carlo was trying to talk with Felicia, and I was hysterical, trying to keep the kids quiet, and Janice helped as best as she could."

"Hopefully, Felicia has some answers today," Sonny said.

I stepped out of the car, bent down, and said through the window, "I'll try calling her again. Either way, I'm going to see Antonio tomorrow."

"Yes ma'am," Sonny said, then pulled away check in with Carlo.

I waved at the valet and the doorman. I was shocked to see DEA agents roaming around my office building. Bad enough they'd trashed our house. "Who's in charge here?" I asked the officer standing at my receptionist desk.

"Agent Roberts. Who are you?" he asked.

"The woman who owns this company," I argued and marched off toward the elevator.

When the bell dinged at my floor, I got off to see James Roberts in my office, sitting at my desk. I walked inside and dropped my purse on my couch. "Do you have a warrant for this?" I demanded, shutting my calendar folder.

He removed his hands and looked up with a raised brow. "We do. Didn't your lawyer tell you we were coming by?"

"I'll be speaking with her soon. What do you think you're looking for?" I asked.

"You can be honest with me, Sabrina. I understand your husband invested a few years back," James said, standing up.

"He has legit businesses and signed up with Washington Finance to invest his funds like anyone else."

"You're the CEO, correct? Taking over from your father?" James questioned, coming around the desk and sitting on the edge.

"You know the answer to that already."

"I can see what Derrick saw in you. Extremely beautiful," James commented, picking the warrant up off the desk.

"Mrs. De Luca, I have Felicia on the line," my secretary Lisa said, interrupting our stare-off.

"Thank you, Lisa."

"I'll let you take the call in private. I wouldn't want your husband's case to get tainted." James chortled as he walked out of my office.

I lifted the phone and turned on my computer to see if any files had been checked. "Felicia."

"Mrs. De Luca, I didn't get a chance to call you; I was in and out of court, trying to get you on the visitors' list," Felicia said.

"What did they say?"

"You can go tomorrow first thing in the morning," Felicia stated.

"Can I come to your office to talk about this in person?"

"Sure, and please don't give Agent Roberts any reason to bring you up on charges," Felicia remarked.

I ended the call, leaned back in my chair, and closed my eyes.

A knock at my door startled me from my oncoming migraine.

"You look like you've barely slept," Lisa said, holding a mug of coffee. She headed to my desk and placed it down.

I thanked her. "Trying to hold it together for the kids and myself."

"They've talked about him all over the news."

"I know, and I hate that because he's a legit business-man, and he lets Carlo and Bruno handle the other business."

"I don't get in your personal business, and I know you've been with your husband for many years."

"I trust you, Lisa; you can be honest with me," I said.

"Do you think they'll convict him?" Lisa asked, sitting in the chair in front of my desk.

"I don't know, and that's what scares me."

"You two have come a long way, and you've always been supportive to me," Lisa told me.

"Thank you, Lisa."

"If you need anything, let me know," Lisa said, then stood up and walked out of the office.

I sipped on my coffee and checked through emails before I left.

* * *

THIRTY MINUTES LATER, I arrived at Felicia's law practice and waited for her to finish her call. I told Sonny that I would call when I was ready, and he didn't have to wait. I planned on having lunch with Janice and Liz afterwards.

"Mrs. De Luca, you can come inside," Felicia remarked.

I dropped the magazine on the table and headed into her office. "Thanks for seeing me."

"Antonio's one of my oldest clients—which means *you're* my client." Felicia told her secretary to hold her calls.

I stepped inside, and she closed the door. "Thank you."

"Please, have a seat." Felicia sat.

"How is he?" I asked.

"He's Antonio. You know him better than anyone."

"I do, and that means he's probably pissed and angry with everybody," I said.

"Indeed, but I believe he's going to get off. I'm waiting to hear the judge's ruling," Felicia announced.

"What is the judge saying?

"He's waiting to hear from Antonio about the names at the table."

"The boss's table—something he can't speak about or risk putting the family in danger."

"Yep. The cartel is very powerful, and you know it," Felicia said, pushing a photo in front of me.

I picked it up and saw two corpses with gunshot wounds between their eyes. "Who are they?"

"From what I heard, they were local DEA agents, working undercover for the De Luca cartel, who can no longer talk about it," Felicia said.

I blew out a breath. "Oh, my God! Are they trying to pin this on Antonio?"

"I'm waiting to hear, but I doubt it because Antonio was locked up when it was done."

"This is crazy."

"I know Antonio didn't kill Camilla. He told me everything, so you don't have to worry," Felica said.

"He said, 'We take our secrets to the grave.'"

"If it meant protecting you, he would confess to everything."

"What can I do?"

"Nothing. Let the Cartel do what they do best and clean up the mess."

"Are you on their payroll?"

"I wouldn't say 'on the payroll', exactly; I changed my last name, but I'm Senator Davis's niece. He has ties to the cartel."

"So, you can get the charges dropped, then. Correct?"

"It's not that simple; no one can know that Senator Davis is involved."

"Then *he* needs to get the charges dropped."

"If Antonio can give up Mauricio, then we can help him."

"He's never going to turn in an underboss."

"I know, and I can't suggest anything that would cause my license to be revoked," Felicia said.

"Understood."

"Good. So, go be the doting wife and visit your husband."

"Thanks. Keep me posted."

"I will. And Sabrina?"

"Yes?"

"Try not to find any more trouble. I have enough to handle with your husband," Felicia mentioned.

I stood to leave her office. I checked the time on my watch and noticed that it was close to lunch, and I'd asked Janice and Liz to meet me. I pulled my cell out and texted Janice to see where she was.

Me: Hey, are you at the restaurant?
Janice: Hey, babe, I'm pulling in now.
Me: Okay. I'll be a little late.
Janice: Everything okay?
Me: I'm leaving Felicia's office.
Janice: Hurry up. I'll order a drink for you.

I closed my messages, stepped out of the office building, and saw Salvatore waiting in front of the limo. "What are you doing here?"

"Sonny called and said he would be late picking you up," Salvatore stated, holding the door open.

"Can you tell me what you know about Senator Davis?"

"Not much, Mrs. De Luca," Salvatore said, starting the ignition and putting his seatbelt on.

"Felicia is Senator Davis's niece; she changed her last name. She thinks Antonio will get off if he turns in Mauricio, but we both know that won't happen."

"Mauricio works for Laurent Carrington, a very powerful family in Italy."

"Felicia said turning in another Don would put a target on our backs," I explained.

Salvatore came to a stop a block from Antonio's, and I felt my phone vibrate in my purse. I pulled it out and noticed a text from Felicia.

Felicia: Antonio is expecting you at 9 AM.
Me: Can the kids come?
Felicia: I could only get you in.
Me: Thanks.
Felicia: He didn't even want me to let you come. I could only push him so far.

I ended the text thread, stepped out of the car, and told Salvatore that I'd ride home with Janice. I opened the door, looked around the busy restaurant, and saw Janice and Liz sitting in the corner booth.

I told the hostess that I saw my guests and strolled over to the table, bending to give them a hug. I placed my purse on the corner of the booth and slid in next to Janice.

I picked up her drink and took a sip. "What's that?" I asked.

"Pink mojito," Janice said.

"I need an IV line with nonstop alcohol."

"What's going on?" Liz questioned.

"Everything. Antonio's in jail, AJ's acting out, and now they're looking into my company."

"Yeah. Gary stopped by and asked me why the DEA was at the office," Janice informed me.

"You're taking on too much, boo," Liz told me.

"I know, but that's what happens when you marry into this family."

"AJ is acting out because he has his father's temper," Janice said, opening the menu as the waitress came over.

"Hello. I'll be your waitress today. My name is Candy."

She looked around 21; maybe she was a college student or something.

"Um, can I have the salad and carbonara pasta?" Janice ordered, and Liz ordered the same thing.

"And for you, miss?" Candy said.

"That's Mrs. De Luca," I spat, rolling my eyes.

"Sorry, I didn't mean anything by it," Candy stated.

"You should know the owner's wife. Just bring me what they're eating, and the same drink."

"Right away, ma'am," Candy responded, grabbed our menus, and strolled away.

"What was that about?" Liz asked, leaning over the table and covering my hand with her palm.

"I'm just exhausted with everything and everybody."

"Antonio will be home soon. You have to have faith," Janice said, taking another sip of her drink.

"What if it costs him our family? I was thinking of moving the kids away."

A loud gasp came from Liz. "What about us and your parents?" Liz said.

"I just want to be safe and not have to keep looking over my shoulder."

"All of us wish we could have that type of life. But Sabrina, you made a choice," Janice told me, taking the plate from Candy as she passed our food around.

I wanted to apologize for my outburst earlier, but at the same time, I was annoyed and dealing with my family in turmoil. "Janice, you don't have to remind me."

"You sure? Because you're giving me an attitude that I never asked to receive," Janice remarked, pointing her fork at me.

"Okay, you both need to calm down," Liz said.

"I *am* calm; your friend is acting like our lives haven't

been changed with Antonio being locked up." Janice dropped her fork on the plate and crossed her arms.

"Janice, you know I didn't mean it. I'm under enough stress."

"I get that, but I'm not your enemy," Janice argued, nudging me on the arm.

I smiled and took a gulp of the mojito, then snapped my finger for another drink. I heard my ringtone. "That's my phone." I took it out of my purse and noticed AJ's private school number across the screen. "Hello?" I answered.

"Hello, is this Mrs. De Luca?"

"Yes. Who is this?" I asked.

"This is the guidance counselor, Patricia Rowland, at the Grandberry Private School."

"Yes, Miss Rowland. Is it Isabella?"

"No, ma'am. AJ was in a fight today, and I talked the principal into not suspending him," Patricia said.

I pulled the phone away from my ear, covering it with my hand and silently cursing to myself. "Thank you for calling, Miss Rowland. I'll be there soon to pick him up."

"Sounds good. I know he's dealing with his father not being home, but we can't tolerate fighting," Patricia mentioned.

"Thank you, Patricia." I hung up, not wanting to go into details of my personal business with the counselor. More than likely, they'll subpoena her and end up testifying against our family.

"Who was that?" Janice asked.

I pushed my food away and motioned for her to let me out of the booth. "The school. AJ was caught fighting."

"My baby was fighting?!" Janice screeched in shock, jumping up and grabbing her purse to take her money out.

"What are you doing?" I questioned.

"I'm going with you. I want to know what dumb little

boy's ass I'll have to kick." Janice tossed her purse over her shoulder.

Liz rolled her eyes and stood to follow us. "I don't know if you should go up there, Janice." Liz commented.

Deep down, I agreed; she might make it worse.

I pushed the restaurant door open and followed Janice to her car.

"Ma'am, has something happened?" Salvatore asked.

"Salvatore, they just called from the school. AJ was in a fight."

"I can take you up there to get him," Salvatore replied.

"I can drive her," Janice argued.

"You've been drinking, and we know how you handle confrontations," Liz stated.

Janice sucked her teeth, aggravated that we all knew how she could get.

"Let me drive all of you, and we can get someone to pick up your car, Janice," Salvatore explained and took Janice's keys out of her hand.

"Get in," I said to Janice, and she flipped off all of us.

Liz jumped in on the other side. Salvatore closed the door and hopped in the front to drive back in the opposite direction of the private school, closer to Broadway and the local colleges. 40 minutes later, we made it to the school.

"Salvatore, I'll be back in a minute," I said as the limo approached the school.

"I wish I brought my brass knuckles," Janice commented.

I grabbed her wrist and headed to the school entrance. I asked the security guard if I could be taken to the guidance counselor. I knocked on the door. She stood up and extended a hand to me.

"Miss Rowland?" I said.

"Yes, Mrs. De Luca. Have a seat."

"This is my friend, Janice."

"Hello," Patricia said.

Janice went to hug AJ and ignored Patricia like a spoiled child. "Are you all right? Let me see your face." Janice lifted AJ's chin and turned it left and right.

"I'm fine, auntie," AJ replied.

"Who was the kid?" Janice asked.

"Ma'am, I don't think that's relevant right now," Patricia interjected.

"I think it's *very* relevant," Janice told her.

"Janice, sit down, please," I begged her.

"AJ, tell us what happened," Liz said.

"I was tired of this kid talking about my family," AJ explained.

"You can't go around fighting people because they talk about your family." I turned him toward me and stared into his eyes.

"He was talking about Dad in jail," AJ said.

"You can't listen to people like that, AJ."

"Is he free to go?" Janice inquired.

Patricia passed me the sign-out sheet, and I filled it out. "Let's go home." I said.

"I still want to know who the kid was," Janice stated and started looking in each classroom. I motioned for Liz to grab her, and we left.

"What about Isabella and Jonathan?" AJ said.

"I might as well grab them now," I agreed. "Can you take AJ to the car?"

Liz nodded, and then walked to the limo. I went to the principal's office to grab my other children. A few minutes later, they were skipping toward the limo in excitement since I had promised them a night at the arcade and pizza.

"Where are we going, Mommy?" Isabella said.

"I have to check in with your grandmother to see how

Enzo is doing, and then we can go to the pizza arcade. Salvatore, can you call Sonny and see if he can get some men to reserve the arcade for us?" I dialed my parents' number as Isabella played with Janice's hair.

"Hey, baby," Mom said.

"Hi. How is my little man doing?" I asked.

"Running around the house, trying to play tag with your father," Mom explained.

"Sounds good. I picked the other kids up early. I'm taking them to the arcade."

"Shouldn't they be in school?" Mom questioned.

"AJ got into a fight." I glared at him as he stuck his hands in his pockets, staring out the window.

"Send him over here, and I'll have your father talk with him," Mom told me.

"Do you guys want to come to dinner tomorrow?"

"Your father has his weekly card game. I may come," Mom responded.

Salvatore turned in the left lane to get on the highway back to Chelsea.

"Keep me updated; we can pick up Enzo after we leave."

"Give yourself a break. We can keep him tonight, so you can relax," Mom said.

"Are you sure?"

"Yes. Are you still thinking about what we talked about?" Mom asked.

"I am, but I haven't told Antonio yet," I said.

"Don't keep secrets from him, baby. Marriages don't last like that," Mom said.

"I hear you."

"Okay. Call me tonight," Mom said, and I ended the call.

"Mommy, has Daddy called yet?" Isabella asked.

"He's still out of town working, baby," I lied again, and I

felt my stomach drop at the sad look on my baby girl's face. "He'll be home soon."

We parked behind another black SUV, and I assumed Sonny had his men come to watch the place. I got out and helped Isabella and Jonathan, and AJ climbed out. "Make sure you two watch your sister," I said. "I don't want her running off."

"Yes, ma'am."

I saw one of Joaquin's men talking with Carlo. I let Isabella down to head inside with her brothers, Janice, and Liz. I started to peel off some money and, they pushed my hand away.

"Carlo, what are you doing here?" I asked.

"Hey Sabrina. I wanted to check on the kids and my wife," Carlo said.

"Your wife is a trip."

Carlo chuckled, rubbed his beard. "I'm surprised she didn't get our kids out of school," Carlo said.

"She was too worried about trying to find the other boy who fought AJ."

"Sabrina, you remember Hugo, one of Sofia and Joaquin's bodyguards."

Hugo extended his palm out.

"Oh. That's where I knew you from."

"I wanted to have someone here who you could trust," Carlo said, as Janice came outside.

"Hi, hubby," Janice cheerfully said, gripping his chin to peck his lips.

"I heard you acted like a fool at AJ's school," Carlo said, tugging on her jeans pocket and pulling her close.

"I have to look out for my babies." Janice giggled when Carlo tickled her around the waist.

"Let me go inside and check on the kids."

I left them making out like some teenage kids and went into the arcade. I saw Isabella trying to throw basketballs into the hoop with Jonathan. I headed to AJ, who was sitting down in the booth with Liz, eating pizza. "Can I join you?" I asked, sliding next to AJ and taking a piece of his pepperoni pizza. "What's going on with you?"

He shrugged.

"You're not a baby anymore, AJ—even though you'll always be my baby."

"I miss him."

AJ leaned his hand on my shoulder, and I kissed the side of his forehead. "I miss him, too. Tomorrow, I'll go see him."

"Were you scared when you found out who he really was?" AJ questioned.

Liz and I made eye contact. "Funny thing is that I ran away from him. Your dad can be a little possessive."

"He used to tell me that you were the jealous one in the beginning." AJ took a sip of his Coke.

"Don't listen to your dad. That man is the jealous one."

"Both of them are crazy for each other," Liz said.

"Well, whatever we are, doesn't mean you go around fighting people."

"I'm a De Luca. We have to protect our family at all times," AJ responded.

"I appreciate you being protective of the family, but violence is not the answer."

"You think Dad would say that?" AJ remarked.

"Finish your lunch and go play some games. After

today, you're on punishment for two weeks. No video games or TV," I stated, and he groaned in frustration.

* * *

LATER THAT EVENING, after my mom came over for dinner, she helped me put the kids to bed, and I showered and got into bed, lying on Antonio's side. I turned the light off, snuggled up with his pillow, and started to doze off when my cell phone rang. I jumped up and checked the time. It was after 10 at night, and most of my friends were sleeping in bed. "Hello?"

"What's going on with AJ?"

Hearing his deep, demanding voice did something to me and brought me back to early in our relationship, and how we were always arguing back and forth about who was right or wrong.

"He's fine."

"You know, I don't like hearing about my son fighting from anyone but my wife," he spat.

"Funny, because it took forever for you to even let me come see you."

"Bella, you know why that had to happen."

"No, I don't, because you keep secrets from me," I argued, pushing the covers away.

"Are you coming tomorrow?" he asked, changing the subject.

"Yes."

"I didn't want it this way."

"So, why not give up who they want?"

"It doesn't work that way."

"Carlo and Bruno should be making those decisions."

"I'm the Don of the family. Every decision goes through me."

"Antonio."

"No. You're my wife, and I love you, but some things, you will not speak about."

"Then let me be clear: My children will always come first."

"They're not moving."

"I can't believe you're fine with being away from us just so you won't break some code."

"It's more complicated than that."

"I spoke with Felicia... Senator Davis?"

"We can talk tomorrow, when you visit."

"What about my company? The DEA took my files. They're saying I could lose my business."

"The government will try anything to get you to turn on the family."

"Yeah."

"Sabrina."

"Huh."

"I love you, Bella."

"I know."

"I'll see you tomorrow, baby," Antonio said.

"Okay." I hung up the phone and walked out of the room. I peeked in on AJ, sleeping in his bed with Isabella curled up next to him.

I had to go to work the next day, after visiting my husband in jail like nothing was wrong. Antonio needed to learn that I was not a quiet woman who would take what he gave me without asking questions.

"You couldn't sleep?" Mom startled me as she came out of the bathroom.

"I just got off the phone with Antonio."

"Come to the kitchen with me for some tea," Mom said.

"How was Enzo today?" I asked.

"He's so full of energy; your father was out of breath

every five minutes." Mom picked up the tea kettle and poured water. I grabbed the cups and bags. "We're not getting any younger, and we love our grandkids."

"I feel like they love the both of you and Maria more than me and Antonio."

She lifted the kettle when it whistled and poured water into my cup. "I know you're stressed about the DEA, and Antonio getting out of jail," Mom said, sitting next to me.

"I don't regret Antonio; I just wished we didn't have to always fight."

"You always have a choice, Sabrina, and you made it when you renewed your vows."

"Why have you never hated Antonio?"

"You're an adult. My opinion about who you love is just that—my opinion. You have to live for yourself."

"What if I want to move the kids away from this if Antonio goes to jail for good?"

"Then your father and I will have to pack our bags and move with you." Mom tapped my hand.

I laughed at her comment. "Thanks for always having my back."

"You're my baby, and your sister works long hours, so I can never depend on her to make time for me."

"So, I'm your backup plan." I frowned.

"Of course not." Mom chortled and finished her tea.

We continued talking about my younger days, and how each of the kids had some of my personality in them.

A few minutes later, I went to take a hot bath and pulled out my wedding photos, and pictures of the kids when they were little. I remembered a few shots of me and AJ when Alex had been holding us captive in Italy. The early stages of my pregnancy with AJ had been stressful, and not only because I hadn't been expecting to get caught up with a man so early. It was super intense and exciting at the same time. When Alex found out about us, he tried to keep us away. Camilla fed into his craziness, and I had to do something; otherwise, Antonio would have never known about his son.

I made terrible decisions when I came back home and tried to protect my heart by not letting him be a father to our son. As always, Antonio broke through and made me see that we were one, and our love couldn't be denied or destroyed. Still, I always wondered what would have happened if Alex never cheated. Would we be married now and happy with kids? I closed the photobook and closed my eyes, soaking in the warmth.

If I could convince Antonio to give up the other man at the table, then maybe we could move on to have some type of peace and happiness.

* * *

"Sabrina, babe, what do you think of this place?" Alex asked, helping me out of his brand-new car and paying the valet $20. It was our one-year anniversary as man and wife. He brought me to this hot Italian restaurant called Antonio's, and I'd planned on us heading out on vacation the next day. Both our work schedules kept us pretty busy, and we were lacking alone time.

"I hope the food's good," I replied, pecking him on the lips, then wiping away my smeared lipstick.

"You know I love you, right?" Alex said.

"I know, baby. You're the best thing that has ever happened to me."

"Same. I know my work schedule has me traveling a lot, but that'll change soon."

The doorman greeted and led us inside. The hostess smiled and asked us how many were in our party.

"Two. It's our anniversary." Alex grasped my palm, brought it

up to his lips, and pressed a kiss there. He had a way of making me feel sexy when he was around, but lately, getting him to notice me outside of family events with our parents was a chore.

I fixed his tie and pressed a kiss to his lips. I pulled back. Suddenly, I felt someone watching us, and I glanced around the room. A tall man with a smirk on his face and ocean blue eyes stared back at me. He must have been popular because everyone was surrounding him.

"Congratulations. Follow me, please," she said.

I looked around the restaurant, and it was almost full to capacity. "How did you hear about this place, Alex?" I questioned, holding his hand.

"Your friend Spencer told me about it when I came to bring you lunch the other day."

"Oh."

Alex held my chair out for me, and I sat.

"Here you two go," the hostess said and passed us our menus. "Your waitress will be with you in a moment."

"I'm surprised they had any openings tonight. Looks crowded," I said.

"Seems like a party or something." Alex held my hand.

I smiled. "What are you going to do first when we get to Italy?"

"Probably sleep; it's a long flight, and I still have work I need to catch up on," Alex said.

"Alex, you promised to leave work here and focus on us, so we can have a baby."

"We're still a year into our marriage, Sabrina; we don't need kids right now."

"Congratulations!" A loud roaring of cheers and laughter could be heard from across the room. I peered over and saw a couple, standing together in an embrace, talking to an older couple. The young girl ran her hand over her protruding belly. She looked to be eight or nine months pregnant.

"Hi, I'm Margaret, your waitress," a voice interrupted me. "How can I get your drink orders started?"

"Yes, can we have a bottle of your best champagne?" Alex asked.

The young woman and I made eye contact, but the look she was giving me made me feel uncomfortable. She whispered something in her husband's ear, and they started to argue.

"Who are they?" I asked and pointed over to the couple.

Margaret turned around to look. "That's the owner of the restaurant, Antonio De Luca, and his wife, Camilla," Margaret said.

"They don't look happy. It's a beautiful thing to bring a child into the world," I said.

Margaret nodded. "I agree, but the rumor is she's cheating on him."

"Wow, that's crazy."

"Not only that; it's with a rival boss," Margaret whispered.

"A what?"

"Another Mafia boss," Margaret said.

"Sabrina, leave it alone," Alex fussed and picked up the menu.

I snapped my fingers. "I knew I recognized him from the papers! Didn't he open a nightclub?" I questioned.

"He did; I'll be back with your drinks," Margaret said.

"That's crazy; I can't imagine dating someone in the mob."

"Good, because you're stuck with me, baby," Alex told me, and I leaned over the table to capture his lips.

AJ

The school bell rang, and everyone went to the classroom except for me and my friends. We ducked into the bathroom. I pulled on the collar of my private-school uniform; it felt like I was suffocating, and it annoyed me. I wanted to burn it. Going to the Grandberry Private School wasn't any different than going to public school. It was actually worse and trying to convince them to let me go to public school instead had been difficult. Don't get me wrong, though; it was better than home-schooling. My parents thought they were protecting me and my brothers and sisters by sending us to Grandberry, but we knew that we were different from other families. It wasn't normal to go around in bulletproof cars with body-guards everywhere. My mom didn't know that I already knew how to shoot a gun. My Uncle Bruno taught me and my cousins, and he said for my 16th birthday, I could go to the gun range and get my own gun.

I was only 13, but I felt like I was going on 30. As the oldest, I had to be in charge while my father was gone and be the man of the house. I didn't know if it was a curse or an honor to be Antonio De Luca, Jr. Either I was being treated like a baby by my mom, or the man of the house by my father. I got into a fight the other day because some kids were talking crap about my dad and showing photos of him from the papers that were talking about our "family of killers".

"AJ, let's go," my friend Jarvis whispered to me as he looked out the bathroom door. Jarvis had planned on skipping class to go hang out with his older cousin, and I didn't want to go, but it was either sit there in a boring class or find something to do to pass the time.

"Did you get the information?" Bobby asked, pushing Jarvis in the shoulder.

They were into smoking, and I wasn't trying to get caught by my parents using drugs and hear my mother's mouth. I wasn't stupid; I knew our family sold drugs, and it would be crazy to get caught taking what my father sold in the city.

"Yeah, man, we can go to my cousin's after we run into the store," Jarvis mentioned.

I agreed, peeking out the window to see if it was clear.

"Let's go; it's clear," Jarvis said, and we ran down the hall and out of the building.

When the alarm went off, we started to run faster and jumped into his cousin's car. Private security pulled up and blocked us off.

"Fuck!" Jarvis said.

"Shit!" I said, knowing my mom was going to chew me out.

"Get out of the car," the security guard said.

"We almost got away, man," Bobby muttered in the backseat.

The door opened, and we stepped out as Jarvis's older cousin passed his ID over to the security guard.

"Do you know who you have in your car?" the security guard asked him.

"That's my cousin, and his friends," Jimmy said.

"Jimmy, I suggest you do research on your cousin's friends. That's Antonio De Luca, Jr."

He shrugged, not really caring.

"Can we go?" Jarvis argued.

The security guard glared at him. "No. This is the third time you tried to skip school, Jarvis."

"Shut up, Jarvis, before he arrests your cousin," I whispered, running a hand through my hair.

"What's going on here?" Principal Spellman questioned, and my day got even worse.

"I caught them trying to skip class," the security guard said.

"Really, AJ? You were just in trouble for fighting," Principal Spellman huffed, pointing at us to start walking back to the school.

Bobby and Jarvis followed with their heads down. We stepped into the building and headed down the hall. The guidance counselor shook her head at me.

The principal opened his office door and motioned for us to take a seat. "I'm calling your parents."

"Why? They're not going to do anything," Jarvis joked.

"Jarvis, you're close to getting suspended if you don't change your ways."

"Man, whatever," Jarvis replied and crossed his arms.

"I know you were caught stealing yesterday," the principal said.

"Can we get this over with?" I mumbled.

"Talk to me, AJ; is this about your father?"

I looked up at him, then glanced at my friends and clenched my fists. "This is stupid." I jumped up and tried to leave.

"Sit down... I doubt your mother would like you being disrespectful," the principal said, picking up the phone to dial our parents' numbers. I hoped she wouldn't pick up, and I could just leave and go stay with my grandparents.

"Are your folks home?" Jarvis whispered.

I shrugged my shoulders. "My mom's at work," I said.

The early morning commute was insane. The guards frisked me and checked my purse as I stood in front of the cameras. All eyes were on me, the wife of Antonio De Luca. I felt a hand graze my inner thigh a little too close to what belonged to Antonio.

"You're clear to go Ma'am." he grinned, stood back, and waved to open the door. I dropped my arms and headed through the gate, looking around a room that was empty—except for my husband. I felt tears in my eyes, and I rushed over to him as he stood.

"Bella." He wrapped his arms tight around me, lifting me off my feet. I trailed kisses all over his face. "Baby, I'm okay. Sit down; we don't have much time."

I gripped his shirt, trying to memorize every inch of his face. "I want you home."

"I will be; just be patient."

"Patient?!"

"Sabrina."

"No! I'm your wife, and this is going on too long. I want

you to turn in his name—or I will." I slammed my hand on the table.

The door opened, and a guard started to step toward us.

"She's fine," Antonio said.

"Boss, you only have 20 minutes," the guard said.

"Wait!" I cried.

"Sabrina, calm down and stop threatening me."

"I want answers."

"Senator Davis's involvement not only traces back to Queen because of her attempt to influence the election in Italy; she also put certain things in place that could have you go to jail for Camilla's death."

"I don't care about that."

"I care!" Antonio shouted.

I jerked back in shock, then rolled my eyes and clasped my hands together. "What's your plan?"

"the judge is on our side, and I'll be set free at my next court date," Antonio explained.

"Are you going to let Carlo handle family business?" I asked, trying to be discreet.

"Things are already in place."

"Why didn't you let me come see you sooner? My mind has been racing, thinking you were being beaten—or worse."

"The warden is on our payroll. I have my own cell, and you know I have a phone."

"So, you think this is a fucking vacation."

"Baby, it has to be this way. I'm never going to be completely out. I just have to move in certain ways that won't justify the DEA trying to bring us down."

"This is all because of me."

"You did nothing wrong."

"Camilla and Derrick were because of me."

"This was all my fault because I fell in love with you," Antonio said.

"You don't quit, do you?"

"If Sabrina De Luca has anything to do with it, then I'll never quit protecting her."

I leaned over the table and pressed a kiss to his lips. "I love you."

"Tell me about the kids and my mother."

"You probably know more than me."

He chuckled at my comment, lifting my palm to press a kiss to it. "I do have eyes everywhere."

"They're fine, besides missing you. Your mom is okay."

"AJ is still coming into his own. I remember living in my father's shadow, and then Bruno wanting to take over the family business."

"He has your temper."

"I know. How is Jonathan doing? My boy was always the quiet type."

"Reminds me of your mother, taking care of everyone around him before himself."

"And Isabella and Enzo?" Antonio grasped my hands.

"Your daughter is spoiled rotten and thinks the world revolves around her. We created a monster."

"She will never have to want for anything, just like her mother."

"I want you home."

He sighed, raised my ring finger. "Bella, you're the strongest woman I know."

"Only because you're next to me."

"That's why I fell in love with you the first time. After getting turned down multiple times, it showed me I couldn't just have what I wanted without earning you first."

"I need this to end now, Tony."

"Bella, trust me."

"Time's up," the guard that was on Antonio's payroll interrupted us.

I leaned in close and whispered to Antonio, "The guard that checked me through the metal detectors got a little too close."

I felt Antonio's hand tighten around my wrist, and his eyes darkened. "What did he look like?" Antonio asked.

"Badge 3458."I stood and kissed him one more time on the mouth, then walked out of the room. As I started to walk out of the waiting room, I heard the alarm go off, and a few guards came over to the guard who was standing next to the metal detector. They restrained him.

"What's going on?" he asked.

"We need to talk to you," another guard stated.

"I can walk myself."

"Don't act stupid, or this can get ugly."

I stepped out of the jail and went to the limo, where Carlo and Salvatore were waiting.

"What happened? We heard the alarm and saw some guards running inside," Carlo said.

"One of the guards got a little too friendly with me."

"Does Antonio know?"

"Yes."

Carlo lifted his cell and dialed a number. "Yeah, she's in the car with me now," Carlo said.

Salvatore drove out of the prison.

"I'll let her know," Carlo responded and ended his call.

"Who was that?" I asked.

"Antonio said you don't have to worry about that guard anymore."

"Why is that?"

"He's dead," Carlo responded.

I smirked, feeling my phone vibrate. I opened a text message and saw Antonio's name.

Husband: Protect you at all times.
Me: Come home soon.

* * *

TWO HOURS LATER, I was back at my office, checking through emails and getting back to what I loved—handling the family business and growing it even bigger. I was thinking of opening a branch in Los Angeles to expand our reach. It was a long-standing tradition and had been in my family for years, so I hoped that one of my kids would follow in my footsteps and not feel like the cartel lifestyle was the only way to live.

"Sabrina, can we talk?" Gary knocked on my door and didn't wait for permission to come inside and sit down.

"Gary, what can I do for you?" I twisted the pen between my fingers.

"This mess with the DEA is not looking good for us."

"Us, or you?" I asked.

"I'm on the board, and you're the CEO. You don't seem to be as concerned as everyone else," Gary remarked.

"Do you understand what I'm going through right now?"

"Listen, I get that your husband is in jail, but that has nothing to do with the board or the stockholders."

"Gary, I'm going to excuse your selfish remark because I know you're not used to this type of media attention."

"Sabrina."

"Mrs. De Luca."

"Mrs. De Luca, you have a commitment to the shareholders and investors," Gary demanded, jumping out of his seat.

"I have a commitment to my family before anything else." I pointed my finger in his face.

"I know your history with Spencer."

My face twisted in a hard glare. "Spencer is dead; may he rest in Hell. But don't think for one minute that I'll be pushed out of my own company."

"All I'm saying is that if this brings on negative media attention, then you should think about selling your shares."

"So, you can be the majority stakeholder?"

"It's something that shouldn't be ruled out."

"Exactly, like I suspected."

"What are you talking about—"

Lisa knocked on my door, ending Gary's questioning. "Sabrina, you have the school on hold," Lisa stated.

I wanted to shrink in embarrassment. "Thanks. Hold my calls," I said.

"Think about what I said, Mrs. De Luca, and get back to me." Gary stalked out of my office.

I sat and picked up the phone to hear what drama AJ had started now. "Hello, this is Mrs. De Luca."

"Mrs. De Luca, this is the Principal of Grandberry."

"Mr. Spellman, how can I help you?" I responded.

"AJ was caught skipping class with some of his friends," Principal Spellman said.

"Where is he now?" I asked.

"Sitting in front of me."

"Thank you, sir. I'll have someone pick him up; I have a meeting I need to get to; otherwise, I would come," I said.

"Sounds good to me. If it helps, he's not a bad kid, like his friends," Principal Spellman said.

I finished the call and dialed Carlo. Even the idea of AJ skipping class and hanging around people that were stealing and were bad influences would only bring more interest to our family.

"Hey, boo," Janice said.

"What are you doing with Carlo's phone?"

"I was walking out of the house, and his phone rang, and I saw your name."

"Are you on your way to the office?" I asked.

"Yeah, why?"

"Gary came here, talking about how I should give up my majority interest in the business." I checked my watch to make sure I wasn't late for my next meeting with a potential client.

"You need me to talk to him?" Janice said.

"No, I can handle him later. The most important thing is getting Antonio out of jail and AJ home."

"What's going on with AJ now?"

"Girl, he was caught skipping class, and one of his friends called his cousin to pick them up."

"What?!" Janice screamed.

"Yes, skipping class."

"See, now I need to beat some ass. He knows better than that."

"Who knows better?" I heard Carlo say in the background. "Why are you answering my phone?"

"Because I can. Do you have something to hide?" Janice spat.

"No, woman," Carlo muttered, and I heard rustling on the other end.

"Take your phone, then. I bet you won't be getting something else tonight," Janice mumbled.

"Stop lying." Carlo chuckled.

I tried to hold in my laugh, but it came out anyway. "Janice is too much." I said.

"Sabrina, what's going on now?" Carlo asked.

"AJ got caught skipping school."

Lisa came to my office door again, and I held a finger up for her to give me a moment.

"I'll drop Janice off, and then scoop him up," Carlo said.

"Thanks, Carlo."

"No problem, sis," Carlo replied.

I ended the call and stood up, grabbing paperwork for the new client and walking toward the conference room. "Is she ready?" I asked Lisa.

"Yes, and I ordered lunch for you all," Lisa told me.

I thanked her and headed down the hallway. When I entered the conference room, I saw my lawyer, sitting with a new client named Linda Dandridge, who we were trying to approach. She came from old money and recently divorced her husband, taking back her maiden name. Linda reminded me of an Elizabeth Taylor type, dripping in diamonds and furs. She smelled expensive. We had money, so nothing really impressed me, but she really stood out with her long blonde hair and high cheekbones. I wanted to make sure my team did top-to-bottom research on her background. She'd brought her attorney along, as well.

"Mrs. Dandridge, thank you for seeing me." I reached out to shake hands.

"I know you're a busy woman, and I wanted to get the details looked at again before I sign," Linda said.

"I'm sorry again about your recent divorce from the senator," I said.

"I'm not," she said and giggled.

"Well marriage can be tough, and you were together for over 10 years, correct?" I probed, pulling out the paperwork for her investment portfolio.

"Michael thought I was blind to his little indiscretions."

"Linda, we should stick to the meeting notes," her lawyer said.

"You're probably right. So, Sabrina, tell me what you can do for me," Linda said.

"Washington Finance can help your money grow. I know you're used to a certain lifestyle."

"I am, and I'm prepared to invest $20 million from my divorce," Linda stated.

"We can break it up into bonds, stocks, and IRA."

"What do you think, Nick?" Linda passed the documents to her lawyer.

He looked over everything and nodded. "Looks good to me," Nick answered and passed her a pen.

"Perfect. If you can flip my money, and I can stick it to my ex-husband in the same breath, then it's a win."

"I agree," I said.

"How about we have dinner, Sabrina? I know you're dealing with a lot; you could probably use some cocktails," Linda said.

"I can't. I'm a mom of four kids; they take up a lot of my time."

She passed the folder back to me. I signed and gave it to my lawyer.

"Oh, well, I can understand that. Kids take up my drinking time," Linda remarked.

I laughed at her statement and held the door open, letting her walk out first. I escorted her to the elevator, and she continued petting her dog.

"Here we are," I said, standing at the elevator and handing the paperwork to Lisa.

"If you change your mind, I'll be staying at the Waldorf until my house is ready," Linda said.

"I'll take a raincheck." I waved as the doors closed behind them and turned to go back to my office.

Janice came in and sat. "I thought you could use some lunch." She held up two bags of food.

"Did Carlo pick up AJ?" I questioned.

"Yep. He texted me after dropping off my food."

I plopped down in my chair and sucked in a breath. "That boy is going to drive me crazy."

"Once Antonio comes home, he'll be fine." Janice opened a bag and passed a salmon salad to me.

I grabbed the dressing and a cup of lemonade from her hands. "Did you talk to Liz today?" I inquired.

"No. She said they're preparing to go back home to Italy."

"I'm going to miss them."

"Me, too. Those boys grow up so fast."

"Just like your three."

"My three aren't stupid enough to play me. See, you're too nice." Janice bit into her double cheeseburger.

"You're like a jail warden, janice," I joked and stole a French fry off her plate.

"I'm hard on them for a good reason."

"Even your daughter," I taunted.

"That little girl has her father wrapped around her finger. She knows when I want to be alone with Carlo, and she goes out of her way to stop me." Janice did an impression of her daughter, fluttering her eyelashes.

"Is that what she does?" I drank some lemonade to keep from choking on a laugh.

"Listen, Isabella is the same."

"Sometimes, I think she's not my child. She says anything that comes out of her mouth, like you." I wiped my mouth with a napkin and stole a piece of her burger.

"Leave my Isabella alone," Janice said. "I'm getting full." She tossed the rest of her trash away. "How did the deal go with Linda?" she questioned.

"She signed and invited me to go out for drinks, but I need to talk with AJ."

"Give him some space. But *we* haven't gone out in a while."

"The kids and work keep me occupied."

"Which reminds me—do you think Gary will be a problem?"

"No. I was thinking of an idea, but I need to see how this plays out with the DEA."

"What are the lawyers saying?"

"Nothing, and I should continue cooperating. They have nothing on us."

"Well, it's a good thing to have Linda in our back pocket if we need her," Janice explained.

"I'm waiting to see what Antonio says first."

"You know, I don't mind bringing out my baby Glock." Janice raised her eyebrows.

"They have enough on us with Camila Queen."

"Anyone that hurts our family deserves what they get." Janice shrugged and crossed her legs.

"Do you want any more kids?" I asked Janice.

She grimaced. "Don't make me sick, please. I have enough trouble with the three I got," Janice replied and starting scratching her arms.

"What is wrong with you, girl?"

"Anytime somebody brings up kids to me, I break out in hives," Janice joked.

"Oh, my God! You're an idiot."

"No, I'm a realist."

"Let me finish working in peace, please, so I can get home to my brats and pray their father calls me tonight."

"Oh, have you had phone sex?" Janice wondered.

"No, and I don't plan on it."

"Missing out."

"I can only imagine the stress you put Carlo under."

"You do realize my husband is the underboss of the mob. How do you think I got like this?"

"I'll call you later, girl," I said, and she waved me off and walked out of my office. I continued to file paperwork, take calls, answer emails from clients and check over the work that my employees sent to me.

* * *

Two hours later, I finished and hopped in the limo. Salvatore drove me to pick up dinner for the kids. I called my mother and listened to her talk about Enzo planting flowers in her garden and making new friends with the kids in the neighborhood, until we got home.

"Thanks, Salvatore," I said and jumped out of the car with bags of burgers and fries. Antonio hated when I spoiled them with junk food, but I wasn't in the mood to cook tonight. I opened the front door and walked inside. Emilia was putting on her coat. "Ma, I'm home; let me call you tomorrow."

"Kiss the babies for me," Mom said and ended the call.

Jonathan ran toward me, and I passed him the food.

"Emilia, thanks for staying later," I said.

"They're good kids, so don't worry. I'll be here tomorrow," Emilia said and hugged me goodbye.

I shut the door, turned, and headed to the kitchen, then removed my jacket and dropped it on the chair.

"Is Enzo spending the night with Grandma?" Jonathan asked.

"Yep. They'll bring him home tomorrow."

"Isabella, come eat!" Jonathan shouted.

"You couldn't just walk to get her?"

"Ma, your daughter is crazy."

"Oh. She's just *my daughter* now."

"I was trying to play video games, and she kept trying to steal the remote."

"Hi, Mommy!" Isabella skipped into the kitchen and climbed into the highchair next to Jonathan.

AJ came in a few minutes later, talking on the phone.

"Make sure you share..." I began, then snapped, "AJ, get off the phone."

"Yeah, she's here. Okay, I'll call you later." AJ said into the phone.

I extended my hand to take his phone. "Give me your phone."

"It's not my fault," AJ argued.

"I don't care. You were caught skipping school, and I told you—two weeks, no cell phone."

"Can I go to my room, please?" AJ asked somberly.

"No, you're going to stay here and eat with us."

"Fine."

"Keep it up with the attitude."

"Dad wouldn't take my phone," AJ mumbled.

"Your dad's not here, and I am. If he was here, disrespect would not be tolerated," I snapped, dropping the phone in the trash and walking out of the room. That boy was driving me to my wit's end, and I was close to sending him to stay with his grandmother or my parents.

I stepped into the living room, grabbed a bottle of wine from the bar, and headed to Antonio's office. I pushed the door open, locked it behind me, poured a glass, and took a sip. I smirked at the photo of me and Antonio at our vow renewal ceremony, and a few photos of AJ and Antonio at his soccer game when he was younger. I ran a hand across the photo of Antonio when he was younger, standing with his father and brother. All three of them wore black suits, and he couldn't have been over 17.

I hadn't been back in his office since he was taken to jail. I stared off into the backyard as the moonlight hit the pool. "He's really in jail," I muttered to myself.

A knock on the door brought me out of my thoughts. "Mommy."

"I'll be there in a minute, Isabella."

I picked up the photo of me and AJ when he was baby. Even being away from him for that year was torture, and now he could be gone a lot longer.

"Mommy!" Isabella screamed.

I sighed and put the photo down, then headed to the door and unlocked it to see Isabella, holding up an ice cream cone.

"Did you finish eating?"

"Yep. Can I sleep with you tonight?"

"Sure, but if you sleep wild, I'm kicking you out, little girl."

She giggled and held her arms out for me to pick her up. I walked back into the kitchen to finish eating and catch up with my kids before they headed to bed.

ANTONIO

*T*wo Weeks Later

The guard unlocked the door and pushed it open, and I walked out with a smirk on my face. He was on my payroll, and I helped put his kids in private school. When I came here two months ago, after this whole thing started, I needed to make sure that I could continue running our business behind bars.

As I walked down the hall, some of my men nodded and clapped their hands in admiration. I slapped hands with Diego of my old running crew from when I was younger. He got arrested for murder. Once he knew I was arrested, he made sure to let the team inside know that I was coming and to have my back.

I can admit that sleeping alone without my Bella beside me every night was difficult, but I continued to stick to the plan I'd set forth when Agent Roberts decided to come for my family.

The guards brought me to Warden Johnson's office. I pushed the door open and stepped inside. He motioned for me to take a seat. The door closed behind me. "Mr. De

Luca, is there something I can do for you?" the warden asked, standing at his door.

"You've done all you can do, warden," I responded, taking a seat in front of the desk.

"Like I said, you have my back, and I'll look the other way." Warden Johnson stated.

"What is this about, warden?"

"I have a lot of things I'll need to clean up, as you know."

I chuckled at his comment. "Have you not been compensated since I arrived?" I questioned.

"I have, but I'm hearing this Agent Roberts has it out for you, and a few fights have happened."

"Fights that I didn't start, only finished."

"Mr. De Luca, we both know no matter what the court says today, your presence has put me in a certain position that I'll need to have coverage for."

I stood up and fixed my jacket. "You're not getting another penny if I think you've gone behind my back."

"I understand."

"Good. I'd hate to have your blood on my hands."

There was a knock at the door, and the guard stepped inside. "It's time, boss," the guard said to me.

I started to walk out of his office, and the strong stench of piss seeped from the walls as I continued out of the jail.

* * *

"Mr. De Luca," Felicia said.

"Felicia. Did you see my wife?"

"I did, and the reporters are in the courtroom."

"What do you think my chances are?"

"The DA is unpredictable, but Judge Ramiro is even-keeled."

"Well, let's go see what the judge has to say."

I stood in front of the courtroom, dressed in a black suit that Sabrina had sent to Felicia. I'd already told Bruno and Carlo to be ready once I left and to prepare for any retaliation. Joaquin had covered his tracks with Queen, but then ended up with Ciro coming after him. That had caused a bigger problem because Mauricio Caputo had devised a plan to steal from Laurent, which ultimately meant stealing from me. The DA and judge wanted names, and we provided one; he just didn't receive the correct information, since Mauricio would be dead before he got brought up on any charges.

One thing my father taught me and my brother was to never let anyone take advantage of the De Luca name. I'd brought this family to the present by running things in step, both legally and illegally. I'd invested a lot of our money into businesses that would only show up to the DEA and IRS as legit. For them to bring me up on any charges of tax fraud meant someone was talking, and I'd bet my money on Mauricio.

"Mr. De Luca, with the lack of evidence, I have no choice but to dismiss the charges against you."

The entire courtroom gasped in shock. I smirked and turned to look back at my family. I saw Sabrina wiping her tears away.

"Your Honor—" the prosecutor began, but he was drowned out by the crowd.

"Quiet in the courtroom," Judge Ramiro said and slammed his gavel down.

"Your Honor, this man is a threat to the citizens of New York!" the prosecutor shouted, pointing at me.

"Judge, I think Mr. Fletcher has a vendetta against my client," Felicia commented, glaring at Grady as the judge tried to get the courtroom under control.

"Miss Marsh, if you have evidence, I suggest you report it; otherwise, your client is free to go," Judge Ramiro said.

Felicia extended a hand toward me before she packed her paperwork into her briefcase.

I walked over to Sabrina and hugged her tight.

"Thank you, Jesus," Sabrina said.

I pressed a kiss to the side of her cheek, then her lips. "Let's get out of here." I whispered in her ear, then grabbed her hand to walk out with my men behind me.

Carlo walked up to us, and I reached out and hugged him with one arm, never releasing Sabrina from my hold. "Brother, it's good to see you," Carlo said, patting me on the back.

I looked around him at Bruno, who was smirking at me. "I see Liz let you out of the house," I told him as he approached, and we slapped hands.

"Lil Brother," he responded.

"I know, Bruno."

"Don't scare us like this again. You know, Mom wanted to come, and I had to force her not to," he explained.

I shook my head, knowing my mother was living on her own after going through cancer, then my father's death, so this was another strain on her that I didn't want to happen. "I'll go see her soon," I replied, then strolled out with my men and saw all the media and the press pushing cameras in my face.

Felicia directed them to calm down, and she'd make a statement.

Sabrina squeezed my hand.

"Mr. De Luca! Mr. De Luca!" the press shouted out.

"The judge made his decision, and Mr. Fletcher tried his best to throw the book at my client and lost," Felicia said.

"What if he brings up charges again?" asked a reporter

from a local TV station that was constantly dragging my family's reputation through the mud. "Are you worried for your client?"

"Grady has no case, and that's all I'll say about that," Felica said, then pushed through the crowd.

I shielded Sabrina's face from the flashbulbs. Salvatore stood outside and held the door open for us. I let Sabrina inside first.

"Go home and be with your kids and wife," Carlo stated. "We can meet up in a few days."

I nodded, climbed in next to Sabrina, and closed the door. Salvatore went around to the driver's side as photographers took more photos of us pulling into traffic. I leaned over and gripped Sabrina's chin, capturing her lips.

"Mmm... Tony," she mumbled.

"I missed this."

She wrapped her arms around my neck, trying to pull me close.

"Are the kids home?" I questioned, cupping both sides of her face.

"They're with your mother," she answered.

"Good." I trailed kisses over the side of her face, then buried my face in her neck as my hand squeezed her thigh.

"Two months without sex; I can bet you're not letting me out of bed for a while," Sabrina said.

"We can get the kids tomorrow. I plan on making up for lost time with your body."

"Promise me something?" Sabrina asked, leaning away from me.

"Anything."

"You'll talk with AJ and keep him from becoming another you?" Sabrina muttered.

I froze at her statement and jerked back. "What are you talking about, Bella?"

She sighed, looking out the window and avoiding eye contact with me.

"Sabrina."

"I don't want AJ caught up in the cartel world the same way your father forced you," Sabrina said, releasing a long-held breath.

"Do you love me?" I questioned, turning her head to face me.

"With all of me."

"Then know that I will always protect you and the kids," I said.

"But we both know he's at a curious age, and I refuse to see my son being trained to give orders," Sabrina spat and jerked out of my hold.

"Bella!" I shouted and tried to grab her hand.

She pushed me away. "No." She folded her arms across her chest and crossed her legs.

I chuckled and started to remove my tie as the limo pulled into our gated home. I ripped the tie off when the car stopped, and I jumped out to hold the door open. "Get out," I demanded.

She rolled her eyes. "Who do you think you're talking to?" Sabrina snapped.

Salvatore started to get out of the car, and I held my hand up to stop him. "Sabrina, I've been locked up for two months without your pussy next to me, and you think this is the time to start arguing?" I asked.

She sucked her teeth and got out of the car. She slammed the door.

I followed her steps with my eyes and smacked her on the ass. "I suggest you be naked in our room in five minutes," I said, and she waved me off. I walked up to the passenger-side window.

"She's scared, boss," Salvatore said.

"I know. Take the rest of the night off, and tomorrow."

"Are you sure? What about the kids?" Salvatore asked.

"I want to pick them up myself."

"Sounds good, boss. Keep me updated," Salvatore remarked, and I passed him a few extra dollars.

* * *

I CLOSED the front door and slid my jacket off, rolling up my sleeves and starting up the stairs to our bedroom. Every step I took, I got more excited about finally being with my Bella again, with no interruptions from the kids or my men calling. I arrived at the bedroom door and pushed it open.

Looking around the room, my eyes landed on my wife, sitting on our bed in only her bra and panties. "What took you so long?" Sabrina asked, uncrossing her legs and standing. She came over to me and wrapped her arms around my neck.

I rubbed my hand across her arm to her waist. "I had to talk to Salvatore."

"Did he leave?"

"Yeah."

"I'm grateful you're home," she said.

"Show me," I replied. I leaned over, and our mouths connected. I groaned in agony as my dick strained in my pants.

"With pleasure," Sabrina said, running her hand down my chest and unbuttoning my shirt. Our eyes stared back at each other. I licked my lips in anticipation of feeling her full lips around my dick. Sabrina helped me out of my shirt and unbuckled my pants, then walked me back to the bed and motioned for me to lie back. Her hands slid into my boxers and grasped my stiff member.

"Baby…" I grunted, wrapping my hands around her wrist and helping her movements from the base of my dick to the tip. She lifted her ass in the air as her mouth teased the tip of my dick. The warmth caused a shiver up my spine. "Damn, I missed this." I held my hand on the back of her head as she sucked me to the base, massaging my balls and twisting the hairs surrounding them. "Shit, Bella!" I groaned. Her nails went across my stomach and up my chest. I was about to come, and I tapped her on the shoulder to stop.

"Mmmm…" she moaned, popping my dick out of her mouth.

"I want to be inside you," I muttered.

She hovered over my body and kissed me on the lips. I pushed her panties to the side, then pushed inside her pussy. "Ugh!" she cried out. The warmth between her legs would always control my emotions, and she knew that. Sabrina had me wrapped around her finger, and I didn't care how weak it made me.

"Fuck, baby, I might come too early. It's been a while," I said.

She giggled, and I smacked her on the ass. "Oh… God, Antonio," Sabrina whispered, dipping her head low to capture my lips.

My strokes were chaotic, since it had been a while for us, but I could feel my orgasm coming soon. Normally, I could have gone for hours to please her first, but now I was about to burst. "Fuck!" I shouted. My dick jerked inside her walls, and I pumped faster, working through my first nut. I wrapped my arms around Sabrina's waist, flipped her onto her back, and ripped her panties off. I dove head-first into her, enjoying my favorite meal.

She lifted her leg over my shoulder and gripped my

head as I dipped my tongue inside and kissed the inside of her thigh. "Baby!" Sabrina screamed.

I continued to suck on her clit and gripped her breast with my hand. "You taste sweeter and sweeter, baby," I mumbled and licked from her pussy to her ass.

"Antonio, I can't take it," she moaned, smacking the top of the bedsheets.

I smirked, pulled back, and moved over to taste her beautiful, full breasts as I eased back in with long strokes. "God, this is home," I said to myself.

"Never leave us again," Sabrina said.

30 minutes later, we both came and fell into each other's arms.

* * *

LATER THAT NIGHT, Sabrina was sleeping, and I got out of bed, covering her with the blanket. I picked up my pants and walked toward AJ's bedroom, then stepped inside.

Even though I was only gone for a short period of time, it felt like a lifetime spent away from him. Everything looked the same, with his posters on the wall of his favorite video games. But Sabrina had told me he was acting out in school a little more since I was locked up, so I planned to have a talk with him soon. He was at that age when he wanted to do everything like me.

I never answered Sabrina's question, but I was still trying to think about whether I wanted to put that type of pressure on him. Even though he was the next in line if he wanted the position, I never wanted to force him into the business.

I closed his door and went to Jonathan's room, seeing his toys scattered around the room. Our second son was more into school, like his mom. We figured he would end up working at Washington Finance when he got older.

I felt Sabrina behind me, wrapping her arms around me and leaning against my back. "Why didn't you wake me?" she questioned.

"You looked so peaceful," I said and turned around to face her.

"Because you're home," she responded, standing on her tiptoes and pecking my lips.

I rubbed her butt cheeks and wanted to be inside her again, but I knew she was tired. "Let's go eat." I said.

"Emilia has leftovers for you."

She turned, and I followed behind her, watching her ass poke out of my oversized shirt that she was wearing. Sabrina opened the fridge and pulled out a pot of food wrapped in aluminum foil. I grabbed two plates and glasses and set them on the counter, watching her move around the kitchen.

"What?" she asked.

"I'm just happy to see you."

"Do you think it'll ever be over?" Sabrina inquired, picking up a plate and cutting a piece of lasagna. She placed it in the microwave to warm it up.

"Let's not think about that."

"Antonio, we have no choice. They came into our home."

The buzzer went off, and I checked the time. It was going on seven, and I needed to make some calls to set things in motion. I grabbed the plate from Sabrina, and we sat down and ate with no words spoken. I lifted my napkin and wiped my mouth, as she poured more wine into my glass.

"I know that look," Sabrina remarked.

I sipped on the red wine and glanced at her flawless

skin. She hadn't aged at all, and no one would have believed that she was going to be 40 in a year. "Drop it, Bella."

"Calling me Bella won't get me to be quiet," Sabrina stated.

She stood up to leave, and I grabbed her wrist. "I just got home after being away."

"Not just 'away' but *in jail,* Antonio."

I sat and motioned for her to come sit in my lap. She hesitated. My eyes narrowed into slits, and a few seconds went by until she came closer to me, and I pulled her onto my lap. "Just let me enjoy you and the kids. Everything else will work itself out."

"You promise?" she asked.

"Have I ever broken a promise, Sabrina?" I questioned, lifting her chin, so she could look me in the eyes.

"These past few months scared me, Antonio. I don't want it to be like this again," Sabrina said.

I pecked her lips once, then twice, and slid my tongue inside. We wrestled for dominance. "Let's go to bed, and then get the kids tomorrow," I said.

We left the kitchen and walked back to our bedroom, then went for another round.

ANTONIO

The next morning, I was standing alone in the shower with the hot water beating on my back. I thought of the time I had spent behind bars. Sabrina worried that I wanted to push her away, but I was only trying to protect her from what was happening in the business side of things.

I had a meeting with the other cartel bosses to discuss my freedom, and what the next steps would be. Since I turned 40, I realized that my focus was more on my kids and my wife. Making money was a bonus, but it wasn't my life anymore.

I turned the water off, picked up a towel, and stepped out of the shower. The face staring back at me in the mirror had a few creases, but I still held my young boyish features. Even in jail, I worked out in the yard without any interruptions. While I was behind bars, the De Luca name had clout, and I was protected at all times, so Sabrina shouldn't have been stressed like she was. No one could bring harm to me; even the warden was scared of me, and we had him on the payroll. Plus, we knew where his family lived.

I rinsed my mouth after brushing my teeth, lotioned my arms, and headed to our bedroom.

Sabrina was talking on the phone; I assumed to one of her friends. "Kimberly, make sure the files are on my desk," Sabrina said, pointing to the clothes on the bed that she'd pulled out for me to wear. I normally wore suits at all times, but today she'd put out a white shirt and black slacks.

I grabbed boxers from the drawer and admired my wife as she conducted business.

"No, I want to sign them this week. Set up a meeting," Sabrina said, standing up and sliding her feet into her pink sandals. I admired the way her toned legs looked in her shorts and oversized cream shirt. I couldn't believe she had four kids and still looked so youthful. "Thanks, Kimberly." She ended the call and slid her phone into her purse.

"Ready to go?" I asked.

"Yes. Did you talk to your mom already?" Sabrina questioned, wrapping her arms around my neck.

I rubbed her back and kissed her on the forehead. "I haven't, but it'll be fine." I pulled out of her arms and picked up my wallet.

We went downstairs as Emilia walked inside with groceries. "Mr. De Luca, you're home!" she said, excitedly giving me a hug.

"How are you, Emilia?" I took the bags out of her hands and followed her into the kitchen.

"I'm good. So happy to see that you're home with the family," Emilia said, starting to take the eggs and bread out of the bags.

"I agree."

"Emilia, we're going to get the kids. Don't worry about lunch," Sabrina said.

Emilia nodded and reached over to cover my hand. "Those kids missed you," Emilia said.

I leaned over to kiss her on the cheek. "I plan on taking the family to Italy for a vacation; I hope you'll join us."

"First one on the plane. Keep me updated and stay out of trouble," Emilia teased, pointed at me.

I grinned, captured Sabrina's palm, and placed a kiss atop it. "Time to bring the rugrats home," I said.

Sabrina laughed as we left out of the house and to my bulletproof SUV. I helped Sabrina inside and went to the driver's-side door. I placed the key in and drove out to my mom's house three blocks over. She lived in a gated community, with my men on watch. At first, she was too stubborn to move back to New York, especially after finding out that her husband had tried to kill her son—something she still had a hard time understanding—but seeing her grandkids grow up was her biggest reason to finally do it.

10 minutes later, we arrived. I showed my ID, and the security guard let us drive up. I helped Sabrina out of the car as my mother opened the front door, holding Enzo in her arms.

"Enzo, look! It's Daddy!" she said.

He waved at me.

"Madre, you look beautiful." I stepped onto the stairs, grabbed Enzo in my arms, and pulled my mother in, too, placing my arm around her shoulders. She put her hand on my chest, and we strolled into the living room.

Isabella was sitting on AJ's lap, playing with her doll. "Daddy!" Isabella screamed. She jumped off his lap and ran toward me, grabbing my legs.

I bent down and picked her up, holding her and Enzo as they squeezed me around the neck.

"Pops!" AJ shouted, running to me. He was almost taller than his mother.

"Daddy, you're home!" Jonathan yelled, jumping up and down.

"I never get this type of reception," Sabrina teased, pouting.

"Stop hating, Mom," AJ told her.

"Hush, AJ." Sabrina waved us off and stalked out of the living room like a big baby.

I sat down to catch up with them all.

"Are you home for good?" AJ inquired, picked up the doll on the couch and passing it to Isabella.

"How is school?" I said, changing the subject.

"Come on, Dad." AJ groaned and tried to pick up the remote control to change the channel.

"Isabella, you and Enzo have gotten so big. I can barely pick you up." I rubbed the top of her head, and she giggled.

Jonathan came around to the back of the couch and hugged me around the neck. I looked up at him and saw my offspring doing better than me, never having to look over his shoulder because I'd do anything to keep them safe.

"I've been good in school, Daddy," Isabella said

I laughed at her statement. "That's good, baby. What about you two?" I asked Jonathan and AJ.

"Straight As, Dad," Jonathan said.

"Good."

"I'm getting As and Bs," AJ mentioned.

"I hear you've been acting out and disrespecting your mother, AJ. Is this true?"

"Dad, it wasn't fair." AJ blew out a breath of frustration.

"And you think stressing your mother out is fair?"

"No."

"Then you'll properly apologize to her, and we won't have any more problems."

"Yes Sir." AJ replied.

"Good because I don't tolerate anyone—not even my children—hurting my wife in any way." I narrowed my eyes and stared at him, so he understood.

"Yes, sir," Isabella, AJ, and Jonathan responded.

"Great. Now, let's go tell Grandma goodbye, so we can grab lunch."

"I think Grandma already cooked," AJ responded.

I stood with Enzo in my arms, and all of us went into the kitchen. My mom was talking to Sabrina and carrying food into the dining room.

"Mother, I told you not to cook," I grumbled.

She waved me off. "Of course, I would cook for my son. I'm happy to have you home," she said.

"Fine, but you'll come to dinner at our house later this week."

Sabrina pulled out Enzo's highchair, and I helped her calm him down after he started whimpering because he wasn't in my arms anymore.

"Hey, I'm right here," I whispered to keep him from causing a fit. It seemed the terrible twos extended to the age of three.

Mother passed the salad and bread to me, then cut the baked chicken.

Jonathan went on about school, and a science competition that he was ready to compete in, while I listened. "Can you come to the school for the contest, Dad?" Jonathan questioned.

I looked up at Sabrina, who was staring at me, and I wondered how I was going to answer. I never went to their school—even though it was private. I never wanted my enemies to know how vulnerable I could be if they had the location of their school. "I'll see, son," I stated and cut up some chicken for Enzo.

"Antonio, I know I can't get you to slow down, but will you take extra precaution now?" Mom asked.

I sipped from a glass of water and let Enzo drink some. "The club is my work, and everything else is irrelevant," I explained, wiping sauce from Enzo's mouth and hands.

"How many more clubs are you planning on opening?" Sabrina inquired.

"Carlo and I have plans to fly to Chicago and maybe Paris," I said.

"When are you planning on this?" Sabrina argued.

"Bella, not now."

"Then when?!" she shouted.

My phone rang, cutting off our stare down. I jumped up and took the call, leaving the room. "Yeah."

"I got in touch with all the bosses, and they're ready to sit down," Bruno said.

"What about Mauricio?" I peeked out of the front window and watched the men post up.

"He's being watched; we can move on him at any time," Bruno remarked.

"Tell Joaquin I will speak with Laurent myself."

"How are the kids?" Bruno questioned.

I felt a presence behind me and turned around to see AJ glaring at me. "The kids are good. Well, your oldest nephew might be mad at me." I heard Bruno chuckle, and I smirked.

"He's you all over again. You want me to talk to him?" Bruno asked.

"No, I'll talk with him," I replied, then hung up and slid the phone into my pocket.

"Who was that?" AJ queried, stepping farther into the room.

"Your uncle."

AJ sat on the loveseat, holding his head in his hands.

"You're angry."

"I want in," AJ said.

"In what?"

"The family business," AJ responded.

I knew this day would come; I just figured I had more time. "Do you know what the family business is?"

"You're Antonio De Luca, the boss of all bosses, the Capo. And mom is the Donna," AJ explained.

I was surprised that he knew so much. "Did you Google that information?" I said.

We both laughed at my comment as I stood over him. "No, my friends at school and I were listening to Uncle Carlo, Uncle Bruno, and you talk," AJ mentioned.

I thought of the times when he would come into my office while I was working or on a phone call. "I never got a chance to be a kid because my father groomed me to take over. He said it was in my blood." I glanced off at the family portrait hanging over the fireplace.

"Were you scared when you killed someone?"

"Listen, I promised myself and your mother that I would do everything in my power to raise you better than I was raised," I said, bending on one knee to look him in the eyes.

"What if you go to jail again?" AJ asked.

"That's not going to happen."

"You can't promise that, Padre. You're not invincible," AJ argued, jumping out of his seat and brushing my hand off his knee.

I'd noticed that he started talking in my native language whenever he was upset with me or his mother. I closed my eyes and composed myself before I could get upset and forget he was my son. "AJ, don't forget—just because you're my son doesn't mean I tolerate disrespect."

"Whatever," AJ mumbled under his breath and started to walk out of the room.

"Stop!" I shouted.

Sabrina rushed into the living room. "What's going on in here?" she asked.

"Nothing. Go back and eat."

AJ kept his head down in annoyance.

"No. Tell me what's going on," Sabrina demanded.

"Baby, not now."

"Antonio," Sabrina muttered.

"Your son wants me to train him to be in the family business."

Her eyes widened. "What?!" Sabrina screeched, gripping AJ by his shoulder.

"Mom, calm down," AJ said.

"Don't tell me to calm down; have you lost your mind? Antonio, I said no," Sabrina told me.

My phone vibrated in my pocket. I pulled it out and saw a text from Carlo.

Carlo: Are you coming to Ryde for a drink?
Me: Yeah, I need to get the kids home first.
Carlo: I talked to Bruno.
Me: He called, and I spoke to him about the meeting.
Carlo: What about the DA trying to bring up charges?
Me: Keep him under surveillance for now.
Carlo: You think he's getting paid under the table?
Me: Possibly. I'll see you in an hour.

I closed my text message. Sabrina stood with a harsh glare on her face. I released a breath and stepped in front of her and AJ. "Did your mom ever tell you about our first meeting?"

"Dad, I've heard this story a million times," AJ groaned, rolling his eyes.

"Doesn't matter; you'll hear it a million and one times if I say so. But AJ, I want you to be a kid and focus on that," I said, rubbing the top of his curls.

"Okay, Pops," AJ said.

"Good. Now, let's grab your sisters and brother, so we can get them home," I said, pulling Sabrina into my arms and pecking her lips.

"You're not off the hook," Sabrina stated, as we watched AJ walk out of the room.

"Really? What can I do to make it a distant memory?" I nuzzled my face in her neck.

"I don't know. I need to think it over."

All the kids came into the living room. AJ was holding Enzo.

"Put Enzo down; you guys spoil him too much," I said, grasping Sabrina's hand.

As we left my mom's house, she held the door open for us and said, "Make sure you call me about Italy, Antonio."

I kissed her cheek and nodded. AJ helped Enzo into his car seat and held the door open for Isabella and Sabrina. Everybody piled inside, and we drove back home.

ANTONIO

$\mathcal{L}$ater that afternoon, I pulled up to Ryde after hanging with my family for a little while longer and taking them to get ice cream. We ended up watching movies and playing board games until the younger ones fell asleep. I walked into Ryde, and everything looked the same since I was last there.

"Boss! Welcome home!" Arlo, the bartender, shouted. He wiped the top of the counter down and slid a bottle of whiskey toward me.

"Is Carlo here already?" I waved the bottle away and let him pour the shot himself.

"Yeah, he's been here for about 20 minutes," Arlo said.

I stood up, gulped the shot down, pulled out $50. I left it on the counter and headed to my office.

"Antonio!" April screamed and ran toward me.

I hadn't seen her in years, not since Ryde opened. "What are you doing here?"

"I'm here with some friends, and I heard you got out. So, I wanted to surprise you," April mentioned.

I removed her hands from my chest and moved around her to leave.

"Where are you going?" April asked.

"April, I haven't seen you in almost 10 years."

"So, we can make up for lost time," April teased, biting her bottom lip.

"I doubt my wife would be okay with me catching up on old times with you."

April twisted a strand of her blonde hair between her fingers and blew me a kiss.

I ignored her flirtations and walked to the office. I opened the door, and Carlo was sitting behind my desk.

"You look like shit," Carlo taunted, reached a hand out to shake.

I sat in front of my desk. "Talk to me," I said.

"I set up the roundtable, and a meeting with Senator Davis."

"When does he come into town?"

"In two days, which gives you time to talk to them and let them know your position." Carlo handed over some pictures of Linda, coming out of Sabrina's office.

"How much did she invest?"

"$20 million."

"Good. Has the DEA found anything yet?"

"From what the lawyers say, they have nothing, so we should continue to let them run in circles."

"Roberts is an asshole who wants to push my buttons."

"But you're not going to give into him because that would look bad, since you just got off on charges."

"I don't have to do anything, but close friends of mine may think differently."

"Antonio, you know as well as I do, we can't go around killing agents whenever we think they're flirting with our women."

"It's bigger than that."

"No, I'm afraid you're thinking of me as a husband, and not a don."

"I appreciate you holding down the fort."

"Everyone is so sure you've cut away from the cartel to focus on being a family man."

"I can never leave it, not after my father's death."

"Do you regret it?"

"Killing him?"

"He was your father, Antonio."

"I'm not interested in going down Memory Lane. He betrayed us."

"Senator Davis only wants our continued support with his investments," Carlo said.

I nodded. "As long as he keeps the judge and the DA under control, then we won't have any problems," I replied.

"Did you see April?" Carlo chuckled

I ran a hand down my face. "She's still trying to be a kept woman."

"She has no idea what Sabrina will do," Carlo said.

I lifted a photo of Sabrina waving goodbye to Linda, then I saw another photo of Felicia and Sabrina in her office. "Felicia said her uncle shouldn't be a problem. The money exchanged hands, and Ramiro is good."

"Mauricio?"

"Kill him."

"You need all the heads to agree."

"They can agree or not; it becomes a problem when my wife is stressed, and by keeping him alive, it only brings stress on my marriage."

"Tomorrow, we meet with the table, and then with Senator Davis after," Carlo said.

"Sounds good. Bruno is moving back to Italy with the kids."

"Janice told me."

"I'd hate to have them grow up away from their cousins, but I understand Liz wanting to have a normal life."

"Unless we can get the girls to stay."

"I'll see what Sabrina thinks about it, but Bruno will do what Liz wants at the end of the day."

"Same as you, a sucker for your wife," Carlo joked, standing and walking to the bar in the corner of my office to pour another drink.

"Make sure we have men surrounding the building, inside and out."

"I'm not taking any chances," Carlo said.

"I need to call my mother," I said.

"How about we have a party here to celebrate you being home?"

"Nothing too big, just family and close friends."

"None of the other families?" Carlo asked.

"Not now. I need to be around people who I can trust," I said, standing and adjusting my jacket. I opened the door and paused.

"Have you talked to AJ?" Carlo asked.

"He's on punishment; I'll talk to him later." I closed the door and walked out of the office. A few minutes later, I hopped into my car and drove home.

* * *

AN HOUR LATER, I pulled up at Sabrina's parents' house. She'd told me they would be there, having lunch. I knocked on the door, and it flew open.

My mother-in-law was holding Enzo. "Tony! So good to see you," she said.

"Good to be home. Is Sabrina around?"

"She's in the backyard with the kids."

I took Enzo out of her arms and tickled his stomach, watching as a wide smile spread on his face.

"He's a sweet boy," Candice said.

"Hi, Antonio," Ashley said.

"I haven't seen you in a while. Where have you been hiding?"

She chortled and strolled over to give me a hug. "Working at the hospital. I finally got away to come and visit," Ashley said.

"Sabrina probably won't want to leave, now that you're here."

"Come in the back. Jonathan is barbecuing," Candice said. She led us through the house.

I continued to kiss Enzo on his cheek as he gripped me around the neck.

"Jonathan, be careful jumping in the pool," I heard Sabrina said. She was sitting under the canopy and drying Isabella off with a towel.

I went over to her and bent down, pressing a kiss on her lips.

"How is Carlo?" Sabrina pecked me on the lips again.

"Good. He's setting a party up for tomorrow at Ryde." I sat next to her on the bench and let Enzo play with his toys.

"He needs a haircut," Sabrina said of Enzo.

We let all our kids grow their hair from when they were born, and when they turned six, they got their first haircut.

"I didn't think Ashley would be here," I remarked.

"She surprised me."

"You seem happier now."

"I'm happy you're home," she said and sat in my lap.

I spread my arm around her waist, pulled her close, and kissed the back of her neck. Her father was on the grill with AJ, and Jonathan was diving into the pool, splashing Isabella. Ashley stood off to the side with her mother, talking.

"Why don't we invite Carlo and Janice over here and just make this a party?" Sabrina asked.

"Carlo has work at the club tonight."

"Maybe next time," Sabrina responded, entwining our hands.

"AJ!" I shouted his name and waved for him to come over.

"What are you doing?" Sabrina asked.

"I'm going to talk to him."

"Here?" Sabrina asked.

"He needs to learn not to disrespect you, whether I'm here or not."

"Yeah, Pop?" AJ interrupted us.

"Sit down," I said.

"What's this about?" AJ questioned.

"Baby, go grab me a beer," I told Sabrina, so she could leave us alone to talk.

"Tony."

"Don't worry; your baby will be fine," I replied.

"Fine," she spat.

I jumped up, annoyed, and gripped her wrist to pull her back into my arms. "Bella, we're just going to talk."

"No cartel, Tony," she said through gritted teeth.

"Mom, that should be *my* decision," AJ argued.

"Boy, you're 14 years old; you get no decision while you're living under our roof," Sabrina explained and marched off.

"Don't speak to your mother like that again, AJ," I warned him.

"She treats me like a baby." AJ leaned back on the bench and covered his face with the towel.

"You know, when I was 13, I was working, earning my way."

"To become the Don one day, right?"

"Something like that. Your mother and I only want you to be a kid right now."

"I'm tired of living like I'm in jail. I want to hang out with my friends and go out."

"Your friends can come to the house," I said, removing the towel from his face.

"Only if their parents go through a background check." AJ fidgeted with his fingers.

"Your mother and I won't apologize for who we are."

"I hear about you in school all the time, and how you should be locked up forever for killing people."

"I'm a businessman, AJ. The De Luca family has ties to different businesses, but that doesn't and won't affect you."

"When I turn 18, if I want to join, can I?"

"What do you think I do?" I asked.

"Give orders to have people who hurt our family killed," AJ muttered.

"I won't lie to you. I have killed people, but the reason has always come down to protecting what's mine."

"Mom."

"Yes, and you. The minute I found out about you, and then you were taken, I had to make some choices."

"Kill or drown in your sorrow," AJ said.

"Where did you hear that?" I questioned.

"I overheard you talking to Uncle Bruno when I was younger."

"Stop listening in on my calls, figlio." I extended a hand to him.

"You rarely call me 'son' in Italian. Pops, are you going soft on me?" AJ joked.

I pretended to shadowbox with him. "I'm Antonio De Luca; I only show that side to you and your siblings."

"Plus, Mom," AJ mentioned.

I motioned for him to lean in closer and whispered in his ear, "Don't tell her that."

Sabrina walked back to us and sat down next to me with a beer and a plate of food. "AJ, you feeling better?" Sabrina asked.

"Do we still have to move?" AJ asked.

I almost spit my beer out. "Who said you're moving?" I peered at Sabrina, and she looked away from me.

"Mom."

"AJ, go play, so I can talk to your mother."

He got up and walked off.

I put the beer and food down on the table. "Sabrina, I'm trying to avoid going off on you, so please explain to me why my son thinks he's moving."

"I only thought it would be a good idea to look into a home away from the stress."

"I told you, I had it already locked in; listen to me sometimes and let me handle things."

"That's easy to say, but all the secrets coming back to hurt our family aren't making me feel secure!" she shouted.

"You blame me."

Everyone glanced at us.

"I blame us both."

"Why?" I asked.

"It's that old saying about the ripple effect. Us falling in love caused so much pain."

"Baby, running away won't fix things."

"Are you guys okay?" Ashley asked.

"Yeah. I'm just tired," Sabrina said.

"I have a meeting tomorrow. Let's get the kids home, so we can talk," I said.

"You guys want to keep them here, so you can be alone?" Ashley asked.

"Not tonight. I need them home, under the same roof," I said and stood up, reaching over for Sabrina's hand. She grasped my palm.

"Call me later, Sabrina," Ashley said.

"I will." Sabrina kissed and hugged her sister.

I led her toward the kids to gather everybody, so we could leave and get them home and in bed. I planned on just relaxing and listening to my babies talk my head off all night.

"Daddy, I don't want to go home," Isabella said.

"Baby, you've been in the pool all day," I said.

"Can I go in the pool at home?" Isabella tried to negotiate.

I grinned at her little wide eyes, looking up at me. "Baby, you can go in the pool next time," I said.She pouted, getting out of the pool, and I wrapped the towel around her. We walked out, with Sabrina holding Enzo. AJ grabbed some leftovers, and we piled in the car to go home.

ANTONIO

The next day, I rode in the backseat of the SUV that Sonny drove, with Bruno up front. I checked my gun in my belt holster, and the one in the hidden side compartment of the car. I had a meeting at my other office, out of which we ran most of the major deals in the city. "Did our men check the area?" I questioned, making sure the safety was on both guns.

"It's secure," Carlo said.

"What about Mauricio?"

"Waiting on you to make the call, and we can go in to grab him."

"We can do it when we go to Italy."

The car stopped in front of the building, and we all stepped out. I'd told the other parties to arrive at 10 AM, and it was 9:30, so we had time to double-check all the entrances before they arrived.

"Bruno, take two men to the back. Carlo, follow me inside."

"Sonny, stay here out front!" Carlo called out.

We went into the building and headed up the elevator

to the top floor. I walked into the conference room and checked to make sure my other gun was still under the table. I bent down and saw it locked in place.

"They're here, Tony." Carlo waved his phone in front of my face.

"Send them up." I took a seat and waited for the rest of the capos to come up the elevator. Five minutes later, Romeo, Geronimo, Umberto, and Aldis arrived. "Thank you for coming, gentleman."

"We didn't have much of a choice," Romeo smugly said, pulling out the chair to sit down. Romeo was around my age, with the attitude of a 16-year-old kid. He was still unmarried and always tried to compete with me and move some of his work into my territory. I let Carlo sit on him for now, but it wouldn't be long before I showed him the old Antonio.

"What's this about, Antonio?" Umberto Costa asked. He was the oldest of the group at 70. His grey hair filled the entire back of his head, but the top was bald. He had a mustache and beady eyes. He was into trafficking and smuggling guns.

"As you know, I was dealing with a little problem with the DEA."

"You were caught." Romeo played with his lighter in his hand.

"We were all sold out by Mauricio."

"Laurent's second-in-charge Mauricio?" Aldis asked. He was the Don of the Calaveras family cartel. They handled most of the cocaine out of Southern Italy.

"If we don't take him out now, then it could be damaging for all our families."

"I think it could be beneficial and make us more money if we cut out the extra dead weight," Romeo announced.

"Romeo, I wouldn't get too cocky. If they can get me, then it's easy to come for you, too."

"I heard this all started with your wife and your side piece," Romeo responded.

I chuckled at his arrogance.

"Wives and kids are left out for this," Carlo said and passed his phone around to show a photo of Mauricio, meeting with Agent Roberts.

"This all goes back to Camilla, doesn't it?" Umberto asked.

"Partially."

"What about his partner?" Geronimo asked, giving Carlo back his phone.

"For now, we can't kill them, but the Judge is paid off, and the DA stopped sniffing around me. But we need to get Mauricio under control."

"Joaquin knows this?" Umberto asked.

"He will, once I call him."

"That deal you guys set in place won't end well for Laurent if you kill his underboss," Umberto told me.

"I'm heading to Italy to speak with him soon."

"So, we just sit back and wait for you to call the shots?!" Romeo shouted.

"I'm the capo, and I don't need to give you the courtesy, but I am."

"Romeo, if I were you, I wouldn't question my brother any longer," Bruno informed him as he strolled inside.

"Bruno, my friend. It's been a while since we've seen each other. Shouldn't you be the one in that seat?" Romeo asked.

Bruno punched him in the face.

"Bruno!" I yelled and waved for Carlo to pull him off before he could put Romeo in the hospital. I didn't need to kill another don, on top of an underboss.

"I can have you taken out for this!" Romeo spat blood on the floor.

"Romeo, you know we don't handle disrespect very well," I said.

"We don't have time for this," Carlo argued.

"I don't agree with this shit," Romeo said.

"I normally don't agree with Romeo, but this could be difficult to deal with if we get backlash," Umberto said.

"Too late; my family is on the line, and I have a meeting with Senator Davis in 15 minutes."

"Wait a minute. Senator Davis?" Romeo questioned.

"Yes, he's part of my plan," I said.

"Mauricio's an informant, and Senator Davis is on your payroll. So, how do we know we're safe?" Romeo asked.

"It's dangerous enough with you wanting to kill Mauricio but bringing in Senator Davis..." Umberto began.

"Senator Davis and the judge will do what I say," I assured him.

"What do you have on him?" Aldis inquired.

"Enough—and I suggest you get onboard. I don't need your permission."

"This is personal, and not business for you." Romeo lit his cigarette.

"Everything I do is business—until it comes to my front door."

"Tony, we need to go," Carlo said.

I nodded and stood. "Excuse me, gentleman; I have another meeting. You can stay here if you need to, but it's done," I said and left the meeting. They continued to argue amongst themselves as I pulled my phone out to text Sabrina.

Me: How's work?
Bella: Fine. Did you get things squared away?

Me: Nothing for you to worry about, Bella.
Bella: Dinner tonight?
Me: I have a meeting tonight.
Bella: With who?
Me: Bella, stop worrying.

I messaged that I loved her and jumped in the car with Sonny, who drove me back to the city to meet Senator Davis at his hotel. He was in town only for one day, and I needed to make sure he understood that if he double-crossed us, then I would personally wipe out his entire family.

"Romeo's getting too bold," Carlo stated.

"He still thinks he controls things, and I need someone to put him down."

"I'd love to," Bruno said, cocking his gun.

Sonny stopped at a red light as a cycler rode through the crosswalk.

"Get me Agent Roberts's address," I announced.

Carlo looked over at me. "We shouldn't move on him yet. It's too hot," Carlo said.

"I plan on having a conversation."

"Little brother, we all know your conversations can lead to shootouts," Bruno muttered.

I shrugged and stared out the window. The car arrived at the hotel, and I jumped out and told everyone to stay in the car.

"You sure we don't need to go with you?" Bruno asked.

"Davis doesn't want to be seen with me; it's best I go alone."

"We'll stay out front," Bruno informed me.

I nodded, headed inside the hotel, and noticed the large crowd lining up at the front desk. It looked like an event was going on at the hotel. I punched the button for the elevator, stepped on, and went up to the penthouse. The doors opened, and I stalked to the penthouse door and knocked.

"Mr. De Luca, come in." Senator Davis moved to the side, strolled in, and looked around his two-story penthouse suite. "Would you like some coffee?" Senator Davis asked.

"I'm here to make sure we understand each other."

"I've spoken to DA Fletcher and Judge Ramiro; you won't have them hounding you anymore." Davis walked over to the TV and turned it onto the local news.

"If you do your part, then I'll make sure your gambling debts are forgiven."

"All $5 million?" Davis asked.

"Only if I stay out of jail, and Agent Roberts finds something else to keep him occupied."

"You never said anything about this Roberts," Davis grunted and took a seat on the couch.

"He's the one who started it all."

"I can't step into an investigation of a DEA agent. I could get brought up on charges," Davis argued.

"I'll like to remind you that your wife divorced you and gave me the information on you using campaign funds to funnel money."

"Antonio, what you're asking is going to put me in a bind."

"Then you should have thought about that before you became Senator."

Davis groaned and held his head in his hands.

"I'm going to see Roberts now," I said. "I want him off my back. Now."

"This won't end with me. Someone else at the agency has your information," Davis argued.

"Then I suggest you get my file and destroy all the evidence," I demanded and turned to leave.

"If they don't get you, then it's only a matter of time until they'll go looking for your wife," Davis mentioned.

"We both know that your ex-wife won't miss you if you disappear." I opened the door, stepped out of the penthouse, and shut the door behind me, leaving him to think about what he needed to do if he didn't want his entire life to come crashing down upon him.

I bumped into the housekeeper on my way to the elevator.

"Excuse me, sir," she said.

"Room 270 asked not to be disturbed," I said, smirked, and stepped into the elevator to head back to the car.

"How did it go?" Bruno asked.

I slammed the door when I got inside. Sonny signaled to the oncoming traffic.

"Davis is testing me, but I have to wait and see," I replied.

"What did he say?" Carlo queried.

"He won't help get Agent Roberts off our backs."

"Should we get some men on Davis?" Sonny asked.

"Yeah. Take me to Agent Roberts's home. I asked Davis for his address to test him, and he refused."

Sonny turned, drove to the freeway and hopped on.

"Is he home?" Carlo asked someone on the phone.

"I can take this hit if you need me to," Bruno said.

"You're going back to Italy," I replied. "I don't need you looking over your shoulder if something goes wrong."

I stared at a photo of Agent Roberts with his partner, sitting in front Sabrina's office building and taking pictures of her. While I was behind bars, I could still access everything I needed. My enemies used the love I had for my wife as a weakness, but I used it to fuel my anger when people tried to bring down the family.

"We're here," Carlo said.

"This is just questioning, Carlo; don't worry." I said.

I got out of the car, headed to Robert's front door, knocked. I saw a minivan in driveaway.

"Hello, can I help you?" A woman with her hair in a ponytail answered the door, holding a baby and feeding it with a bottle.

"I'm looking for James Roberts."

"Who are you?" she questioned.

"Tammy, who's at the door?!" I heard Roberts called out.

"De Luca," I offered.

"Some guy named De Luca!" she called back.

James came to the door in uniform and pushed her to the side. "What are you doing at my home?" James asked.

"I was in the neighborhood. I'm thinking of buying property."

"Something tells me that's a lie."

"So is you living in this house, which I estimate runs about half a million dollars."

"What's going on, James?" Tammy asked.

"Nothing. Go back in the house."

I slid my hands into my pockets.

"Mr. De Luca, I know you think you're scaring me," James said.

"Is that your wife?" I asked to push his buttons.

"None of your business." James narrowed his eyes.

"I mean, I have kids myself, so I could understand having a busy job that keeps you away from your family."

He chortled and ran his thumb over his nose. "The case won't be dropped. You can bring your men over here to intimidate me, but it won't work," James said.

"Then I guess you've figured me out."

"DA Fletcher and the judge might think you're innocent, but I don't," James said.

"My wife's company has nothing to do with your investigation."

"And if I don't stop?" James asked.

"My wife is looking for more property to invest in; this area is looking lovely."

"So, you think moving in would scare me?" he questioned.

"I don't need to scare anyone, Agent Roberts. You need to realize I run this city."

"Are you threatening me, motherfucker?!"

"James!" I heard Tammy scream, and James took off toward her.

I stepped inside, looking around at all the mess from the toys and clothes scattered around. It looked like they either just moved in or were moving out. Boxes sat on top of the table near the kitchen.

"I thought I saw someone out back." Tammy clung to James's waist.

"It's just the groundskeeper," James stated.

I leaned against the door. "I could have my guy that cuts my lawn come see you."

"Get the fuck out of my house!" James shouted, and the baby started to cry. James started to walk toward his bedroom.

I held my hand up. "I wouldn't think about getting a gun, Mr. Roberts. I have my people surrounding you."

"James, what's going on?" Tammy whimpered, pulling on his arm.

"Nothing. Go to our room and call the police," James said.

"Tammy, if you want to see your husband again, then I wouldn't move."

"Oh, my God!" she cried out.

"That's enough. Get out of my house." James moved in front of Tammy.

"I understand your friendship with Derrick; you want to avenge his murder," I calmly replied. "But don't get yourself hurt."

"Just leave, please," Tammy demanded and hugged her child close.

"My two-year-old has the same pajamas," I said and walked out with my back to them, not worried about him calling the police. If Senator Davis did his job, then I wouldn't hear from Roberts ever again.

I'd surprised Antonio with a hotel room for the night, so we could be alone without the kids before we got too deep into work again. I had the entire room decorated with candles, and his favorite foods. I wore a red lingerie set that was edible, and he ripped it right off me, not sparing a moment. He then carried me to the bathroom. Everything was set up in our large tub, with bubbles and flowers surrounding us.

I watched the bubbles cover my perfect skin as he pumped in and out of me. My stomach was in knots, and my eyes were rolling into the back of my head. Antonio was so deep; I could barely breathe.

"Agh... shit!" he cried.

"Antonio... please." I gripped his neck.

He pumped faster and faster as the water splashed around the tub.

"I missed this!" I cried out, pressing a kiss on his lips, his cheek, and the back of his ear.

He bent down, grasped my breast, and squeezed,

flicking his tongue across my nipple, then tweaking it. "Damn, this is the best pussy," Antonio groaned.

I held the back of his head as he sucked each breast tenderly. I moaned as Antonio slipped a finger in my ass, and I started to tremble in his arms. "Ahhh... baby..." I gasped. My head fell back, and my mind released every worry I was dealing with.

"Tell me who you belong to," Antonio said, lifting me out of the tub.

"Wait... don't drop me!" I screamed, tightening my arms around his neck. My body felt like it was floating in the air.

"Mmmm... who do you belong to?" Antonio questioned again, walking us to the bedroom and placing me atop the bed. He placed the finger he'd used to penetrate me into his mouth and sucked the juices off.

"You. Oh, God, baby," I panted as he tightened his hold on my waist, slamming in and out. My mouth fell open at the pleasure and pain.

He shoved his tongue down my throat, and I raised my leg around his waist. I pulled him farther into me as he breathed into my mouth. He bit my bottom lip, and I groaned as his head dipped down against my breast. "I swear to God; I'll kill for you, Bella," Antonio stated.

I reached down to push him away, and his eyes darkened as I took control. I winked and turned to kneel in front of him. I pointed for him to lie on his back. "I want to taste you."

"Bella," he moaned when my lips teased the tip of his thick girth. One of the things that we used to love to do early in our relationship was please each other with oral sex to see who could come first.

"Ouch!" I yelled as he smacked my ass, rubbed the sting away, and pulled my legs across his body to adjust my pussy directly over his mouth.

"Feed me, baby." Antonio's gravelly voice sent shivers up my spine.

I felt his fingers digging into my skin, kneading my butt cheeks and thighs. I inhaled a sharp breath when his tongue entered my ass. He smacked, squeezed, and kissed my ass. Our intimacy had grown even more over the years, and he knew my wants and needs. I gazed at his fully erect penis and spit on the tip, then closed my mouth around its fat, mushroom-shaped head.

"Ahhh!" Antonio breathed.

I stopped sucking, and I felt his eyes on me. He started thrusting upward, and a few minutes later, he shot down my throat. I moved up to the head of the bed and devoured his lips. His arms tightened around me as we made out.

"I love you," Antonio said.

"I love you more." I rubbed my nose against his as we stared into each other's eyes.

* * *

Two Days Later

The door of my office burst open, and Agent Roberts stood there with a hard glare on his face. His clothes looked dingy, and he was unshaven.

"Can I help you?" I asked.

"I think it's interesting that you send your thug husband to do your dirty work," James stated, throwing some papers on my desk.

"What's this?"

"I was told to close the case on your company, and I got a feeling you knew that already."

"I don't understand." I picked up the paperwork and it read that James Roberts was no longer a part of the DEA.

"Your husband just happened to stop by my home and threaten me," James said.

"Antonio wouldn't do that."

"Bitch!" James tried to charge at me.

I pulled out the gun that I kept in my desk drawer. "Mr. Roberts, I suggest you get out of my office before I blow your head off."

He bent over in laughter. "This is far from over," James said.

Lisa stormed in with security. "You need to leave, sir," Lisa said.

"I'm not going anywhere until she admits what she did," James says and took a step toward me.

I took the safety off the gun. "Manny, please escort Mr. Roberts off my property. If he resists, then shoot him," I said.

"You're just like your husband," James explained. "That innocent act doesn't fool anybody."

Manny grabbed both his arms and started to put him in a headlock.

"I've never pretended to be innocent," I said. "I just have a better way of controlling my temper—unlike my husband."

"De Luca will get his one day," James said.

"That day won't be today," I answered. I lowered my gun, put the safety back on, and slid it back into the drawer.

"Do you need me to do anything?" Lisa asked.

"No, I'm fine. Thanks, Lisa." I picked up the office phone and called Antonio. I sat back in my chair, reading through the documents. One was about ending the investigation, and the other was about James getting fired. I'd never imagined Antonio would go to his home and threaten him.

"Bella." Antonio sounded out of breath.

"What are you doing?" I asked.

"Where is he?!" Janice burst through the door with a bat.

"Janice, he's gone."

"Who's gone?" Antonio asked. "What's going on, Sabrina?"

I snapped my fingers at Janice to get out. "James Roberts just showed up here."

"He doesn't listen," Antonio said.

"Leave it alone; he was fired," I replied.

"I'm sending Sonny to check on you."

"What are you doing?" I questioned.

"I'm at the club."

That meant he was probably holding a meeting that wasn't really about the club. "What time is our flight tomorrow?" I asked.

"I'll have the jet ready at 6 AM," Antonio said.

I groaned, thinking of having to get the kids up early to fly. "All right. Let me get back to work."

"Are you sure you're okay?" Antonio asked.

"Yes. Don't send Sonny; I don't need anything."

"I'll pick you up from work today."

"You rarely pick me up anymore," I said.

"Bella, don't start," he sighed.

I giggled and sat back, crossing my legs. "You don't flirt with me anymore."

"What are you talking about?" he questioned.

"We used to have phone sex, and quickies. Are you getting too old, honey?" I taunted, licking my lips and thinking that he was probably ready to storm over here.

"Bella, don't play with me," Antonio grunted.

"Try not to do anything else to get on Roberts's radar. What about his partner?"

"Right now, he's quiet, and I expect him to stay that way if he wants to continue to have a pension," Antonio said.

"I'll see you when you pick me up," I said, folding the paperwork and putting it into my purse. I heard the dial tone and put the phone on the cradle to file the rest of the day's paperwork away.

Lisa placed a stack of folders on my desk, and I shook my head, thinking about the numbers I'd need to calculate and input to make sure my investments were legit. Some companies didn't pay attention to incoming and outgoing accounts. But I couldn't have any dummy corporations attached to my family's name.

I piled them up and put them in my briefcase to read over on my trip to Italy tomorrow. I picked up my phone and saw a text message from Antonio.

Husband: I can help you join the mile-high club.

ANTONIO

At 6 AM, I carried a sleeping Enzo in my arms with his favorite blanket around him as AJ, Jonathan, and Sabrina walked ahead of me. Sonny was carrying Isabella, who kept crying because she was disturbed from her sleep. I rubbed Enzo's back and stepped onto the jet, walking him to the back bedroom with Sabrina. Sonny laid Isabella down, then helped take off Enzo's shoes and jacket. He was knocked out cold, and Sabrina kissed him on the forehead.

"I'll be out in a second," Sabrina said.

I pecked her on the lips. She was the first one awake after working late last night and packing the kids' bags. We'd had a family dinner, and she called her parents and sister to let them know that we would be out of the country for a few weeks. Carlo and I weren't only coming to see Laurent and Mauricio but to see how our club was running, too.

"Sir, we are ready for takeoff," the flight attendant said, passing the boys blankets and pillows, so they could get comfortable.

"Thanks, Luann."

"Dad, how long is the flight?" Jonathan asked.

"A few hours, so get some sleep," I said and sat across from my mother.

"I haven't been back since your father," my mother remarked.

"I come for business but mostly stay away from the old house."

"It's better left that way. At one time, he was a good man," my mother explained.

"I know."

"When is Bruno coming?" my mother questioned.

"He's flying with Liz and Carlo," I said. I felt a hand on my shoulder, and I looked up. It was Sabrina, standing next to us. "Are the kids good?" I questioned.

"Yeah, Isabella finally stopped whining." Sabrina sat in the chair next to me.

"We have a second bedroom if you want to go rest," I said to my mother.

"I'm fine here; you two go relax."

The pilot came on the intercom, and the doors closed as the plane started to head to the runway.

Sabrina covered her mouth and yawned. I stretched the blanket out to cover both of us. She leaned her head against my shoulder.

"Get some rest," I said.

"I will," Sabrina responded, kissing me on the cheek.

The flight attendant turned out the lights. They boys were lying back in their seats, snoring.

A day later with the time change, we arrived at our airstrip to our waiting limos. I tapped Sabrina on the leg, and her eyes fluttered open. I tried to press a kiss on her lips, and she covered her mouth to stop me.

"What are you doing?" Sabrina asked.

"Give me a kiss."

"No, I need to brush my teeth first."

"I don't care about that; I've kissed every part of your body."

She smacked me on the arm, and I chuckled. "Keep your voice down," she demanded.

"We have arrived at our destination," the flight attendant said, walking down the aisle to grab the pillows and blankets.

"I'm hungry," Jonathan said.

"We can get food when we get to the house," I replied.

"When was the last time we came to Italy?" Jonathan asked.

"You were a baby, like Isabella, and probably don't remember," Sabrina said, jumping up and going to the back of the plane.

"AJ, wake up," my mother said, unbuckling her seatbelt.

The door opened, and Carlo stuck his head inside. Sonny woke up and helped grab the bags.

"Uncle Carlo, can I stay with you and Auntie?" AJ asked, and I shook my head.

"I'll talk to your mother," Carlo said.

"No, he's going to stay with us," Sabrina responded, coming out of the back room with Enzo in her arms. He was wide awake, eating an apple.

"I'll get Isabella," I said. I walked into the bedroom and saw Isabella leaning up against the headboard, with her eyes closed, and her hair all over her head, with one pigtail sticking up. "Sweetheart, we're here."

"I want to go home," Isabella whined.

"We are home—your other home in Italy."

"No, Daddy. I want my friends." She started to wipe the tears on her cheeks away.

I kissed the top of her head, lifted her palm, and

pretended to eat her hand. "Pumpkin, relax; we'll have your favorite food ready when we get home."

I finally got her to calm down, and we piled into the limos and drove to our house.

* * *

AN HOUR LATER, we arrived, and I helped Sabrina get everyone situated. We had housekeepers who lived on the grounds to help keep things updated, and Emilia arrived with Bruno and Carlo. She went straight to the kitchen to start cooking. I put Isabella in her room, while AJ and Jonathan went to go play video games. I walked to the bathroom and started the shower, taking off my jacket, pants, and shoes.

"How long will you be?" Sabrina asked, standing against the sink counter as I undressed.

"Not long; we need to talk with Laurent," I replied, heading to her and pressing my body against hers.

She gasped in shock at my arousal; I was hoping to get in a quickie before I had to leave. "We can't; the kids are still awake," Sabrina said.

I trailed kisses over her shoulder. "My mother can get them."

"Mmmm…" she moaned, putting her hand on the back of my neck.

"I feel like we've been working on opposite schedules," I said.

"I know."

"After this meeting, we can have alone time, just the two of us."

"Maybe outside on the patio," Sabrina stated, sliding her hand down and gripping my erection.

A knock on the door interrupted us. "Daddy! Where's Mommy?" Isabella called out.

"Your daughter needs you," I said.

"If we stay quiet, maybe she'll go away," Sabrina joked.

"Daddy! What are you doing?" Isabella banged on the door.

"A quickie is out of the question now." I completely went soft, stepped back from Sabrina and stepped in the shower.

Sabrina giggled and walked toward the door. I peeked my head out and saw Isabella, holding Enzo's hand and talking to their mother. "What can I help you with, Isabella?" Sabrina questioned, turning them around to walk out.

"I want to go shopping," Isabella said.

I shook my head. She was spoiled rotten, and I couldn't say I was sorry for doing it.

* * *

AN HOUR LATER, I came downstairs to the living room to see Carlo and Bruno, talking to AJ and Jonathan.

"Are we ready to go?" I asked.

"All set, little brother," Bruno said.

"Janice and the kids went with Sabrina and Liz to lunch and shopping," Carlo mentioned as we stepped out of the house.

"Emilia cooked for them already," I said and slid into the car.

"Isabella wanted to shop, and Janice encouraged her, so Sabrina lost." Carlo laughed.

Sonny shut the back door, and we headed to the meeting with Laurent.

"Have you spoken with Joaquin?" Bruno questioned, turning in his seat to face me.

"I haven't yet; I'll call him after this meeting," I said.

I noticed another car following us; it was the same make and model that Laurent's people usually drove. They didn't know we'd be in town until the last minute.

"You think Mauricio knows we're onto him?" I asked.

"I doubt it because he's been wrapped up in women and using the same drugs he's selling," Carlo replied.

"Sonny, make a right turn at this corner," I said, trying to see if what I was thinking was true. Laurent would never jump the gun and try to come for the Don of another family. Mauricio, on the other hand, would do anything to keep his secrets covered up. Sonny made the turn and sped up, and the same car followed us and speed up. I looked up and saw a gun in my peripheral view. "Fuck!"

"What's up?" Bruno said.

"I think Mauricio's men are tailing us."

"Sonny, take the next exit," Bruno directed.

"Hold on," Sonny said.

I lifted my gun and checked the chamber for bullets. Suddenly, I felt the car bump into us and try to push us off the road. "Carlo, take the left, and I got the right."

We were in a bulletproof car but getting us to crash would be the biggest story in Italy. Sonny made another sharp turn and avoided hitting a young boy on a bike. He sped up and sideswiped a car, and I stuck my hand out and started shooting at the car behind us. The car sent bullets toward us, and I ducked down. Bruno aimed his shotgun and blew the side mirror off. Another shot went off, and he hit the tire. They sped out of control and hit a parked van.

"Sonny, pull over here," I said.

He stopped the car, and I got out with Carlo and Bruno next to me. I kept my gun aimed high as we eased to the car. Both men were slumped over in the car. Smoke was coming from the engine. I yanked the door open and checked the driver's pulse. Carlo did the same for the passenger, and both were dead. Blood trailed down their faces.

"Laurent's men," Carlo said, showing a tattoo of the Carrington cartel on his knuckle.

"He wouldn't be this stupid to come for me. What if my family were with me?"

"Try and stay calm, Tony," Carlo said.

"These motherfuckers really think I'm going to be played with?" I lifted the gun and shot him in the head to send a message.

"We need to get out of here before someone sees us," Carlo said.

I nodded, checking his pockets and grabbing his wallet. We ran back to the car and headed to the meeting. I looked at the ID and address. His last name was Caputo. I grinned, knowing Mauricio would be seeing me soon.

THIRTY MINUTES LATER, we made it to Laurent's cafe. It was a front for his casino downstairs, and where he held most of his meetings. I got out of the car and followed Carlo inside. They wanted to pat us down for guns, and I smacked their hands away.

"It's okay fellows!" Laurent called out. He was sitting in the back corner. The place was closed.

"Laurent, explain to me why I shouldn't kill you right now," I demanded.

"Mr. De Luca, take a seat," Laurent said.

I pulled out the wallet and placed it on the table, sliding it over to him.

"What's this?" Laurent asked.

Carlo and Bruno stood on both sides of me for protection. "You tell me," I replied. "A wallet from the gunman that I took after putting a bullet in his head."

Laurent picked up the wallet and checked the ID. "You killed him?" Laurent asked.

"It was either him or us," Carlo responded.

"I got your message. You wanted to meet," Laurent said.

"I'm killing Mauricio, and I don't care if you're against the decision."

Laurent looked from Carlo to me and folded his hands in front of him. "Why?" Laurent asked.

"He's a mole, Laurent." I sat back in the chair.

"I don't believe you."

"I figured you wouldn't." I pulled out my phone and scrolled to the photos of James and Mauricio. I placed the phone on the table and pushed it toward him.

"He's the reason you were arrested?" Laurent asked.

"More than that; he went after my wife, and you know how I feel about that." I sneered, swiping my phone away fast.

"Antonio, I apologize for what was done," Laurent said.

"Save the apology. This is a courtesy, but I don't need your permission."

"Romeo and Umberto did call, but I never got the message," Laurent said.

"Mauricio probably intercepted the messages," Carlo explained.

"Where is he?" I asked.

"At the warehouse; he finished a deal with the Russians."

"Give me the address."

"How many men did he take with him?" I questioned and started to stand.

"He's my underboss, Antonio."

"Pick them better next time. Text Carlo the address,

and I'll be in touch soon," I said and strolled out of the building.

We got back in the car, and a few minutes later, Carlo's phone vibrated. Sonny headed over to the address that he typed into the navigator system.

"Bruno, call some men for backup." I checked the time on my watch and called to see how Sabrina was doing.

"Hey, babe," Sabrina said.

"Where are you?"

"Finishing up shopping and heading to lunch," Sabrina said when I heard some rustling on the other line.

"Mommy! That man pushed me!" Isabella cried out.

I sat up. "Sabrina! What the hell is going on?"

"Let her go!" Sabrina screamed.

I almost lost my mind. "Sonny, change directions; track Sabrina's car!" I yelled.

Everyone looked back at me in panic. "Where's Janice?" Carlo asked.

I tried to hear what was going on.

"Bitch, I'll shoot you if you move an inch," I heard a deep voice say.

"Do you know who I am?" Sabrina challenged him. "If you did, then you'd know my husband will kill you before we even get in your car."

I kept calling her name on the other line. "Sabrina!" Then I said to Bruno, "Call Laurent; he must have tipped him off."

"Boss, we're five minutes away."

"Bruno, I want their heads."

The car sped in and out of traffic as I kept them on the phone to hear them arguing. On the GPS, we noticed they were at the corner ice cream shop, next to the doll store. We finally pulled up and noticed a group of men surrounding Sabrina and my scared daughter. Janice had a gun to her head.

I glanced at Carlo, and he held a hard grimace. "Bruno, you get the kids out of here. Don't kill anyone out here," Carlo said, taking the safety off his gun.

"I want them dead now," I demanded.

"Tony, we can't do that in broad daylight and in front of our kids," Carlo reminded me.

I nodded, massaging my temple. My temper was rising high from seeing someone's filthy hands on my daughter.

The car stopped abruptly in the middle of the street, and we hopped out, pointed our guns at the six men. The one who I assumed was the leader started laughing.

"Let her go."

"I heard you have a beautiful wife and daughter; I had to see for myself," he said.

"Did Mauricio send you?" I questioned.

"The boss wants to send a message," he stated, gripping Isabella tighter.

"Let my daughter go, and I'll let you walk away."

"What about them?" the one in charge replied, pointing to Carlo and Bruno.

"They won't touch your men if you let our women go."

"I kind of want to see what all the fuss is about. I could be a husband and father," he said, ruffling Isabella's hair.

Sabrina tried to charge him, and he held the gun to her head.

"Bella! Stay back," I demanded.

"Antonio," Sabrina spat, narrowing her eyes.

"I'll make a deal with you," the gunman said to me. "We leave them alone, and you stop the hit on Mauricio."

"I don't answer to you."

"Antonio!" Sabrina turned an angry glare at me.

"Bella, listen to me." I stared into her eyes.

"Let my daughter go," Sabrina said.

I glanced at Janice, Carlo, and Bruno, making eye contact.

"Bruno," I muttered, closing my eyes for a second.

Gunshots went off above our heads, and the entire crowd screamed and pushed each other to get to safety. The gunmen were surprised and started to send shots back toward us. I saw Sabrina lunge and grab Isabella. Janice bit the arm of the man who was holding her. Carlo got off a shot. Janice pulled her gun out and started shooting.

I ran to Sabrina and Isabella as the crowd started to disperse. "Bella! Bella!"

"Here, Tony!" Sabrina screamed.

I rushed toward them and covered them with my body. I lifted my head and watched as two of the five men jumped in a car and drove off. Sonny was by my side to pick up Isabella as she cried, and I helped Sabrina up. "You okay?" I asked, checking her over from head to toe.

"No, but I will be," she replied.

"I'll have Sonny take you home," I said.

Another car pulled up, and my men jumped out.

"We need to get to Mauricio now," Bruno said.

"I'm coming with you," Sabrina said.

"You need to go with Isabella," I argued.

"Janice can take her home."

I sighed, running a hand down my face. "Sabrina."

"No, Antonio, I'm going with or without you. The kids can ride with Sonny," Sabrina explained.

"Carlo, do you have an extra gun?" I asked.

All the kids and Janice piled in Sonny's car.

I hugged Sabrina tight around her waist and kissed her on the mouth. "I want you to follow me and don't speak."

"I promise," Sabrina said.

I chortled because we both knew she could never

promise anything like that. "Get in the car." I walked over to the limo and checked on Isabella. She clung to Janice, and I wanted to make sure that she knew I wouldn't let anything happen to her. "Sweetheart."

"Daddy!" Isabella cried.

"I'm sorry, baby. It won't happen again."

"Make sure Carlo is safe, Tony," Janice said.

I kissed her cheek. "You know I will."

"Come home, Daddy," Isabella begged.

"I'll be there soon, right behind you," I replied, hugging her tight and kissing her forehead.

"We need to go," Carlo interrupted. "Mauricio got word that his hit didn't take."

I nudged Isabella to go back to Janice, then I shut the door and ran toward the other car. I jumped in and cupped Sabrina's face. "You good?" I asked, peering into her eyes.

"I will be when he's dead. We haven't even been here one full day," Sabrina fussed and rolled her eyes.

"I'll make up for it later."

She leaned over and bit my bottom lip, then sucked on it.

I groaned, feeling my dick stiffen in my pants. I cleared my throat. "Later, Bella," I said.

The car left the scene as the police started to pull up and get information on what went down. I'd get a call from the chief later, and I expected to have to pay him off to keep it quiet.

* * *

An hour later, we arrived at an abandoned furniture store that Laurent had turned into an import-export business. There weren't any cars out front, and I expected them to know we'd show up, so they were probably sitting and waiting inside.

I took the gun out of the glove compartment and passed it to Sabrina. "Just in case."

"Always," she responded and grabbed it.

"We don't know how many people he has inside with him," Carlo stated.

"How much longer for backup?" I asked.

Bruno glanced at his phone. "Paulo is 10 minutes out."

Gunshots went off.

"Sabrina, get back!" I shouted and pushed her behind me.

"That bastard might have people everywhere," Carlo spat, sending shots back to the top-right window.

More broken glass. I covered Sabrina while sending shots in all directions. There was a loud screech, and multiple SUVs pulled up and blocked us to get a better angle. It was Paulo, and some of our men.

"There here!" Bruno yelled and grasped another gun from Paulo.

Sabrina pushed my hand away, sent off a shot to the front door.

"Let's take the side door," I told my team.

Sabrina followed. I wasn't letting her out of my sight. We stayed against the wall of the building, and I peered into the window nearby and saw a few of Mauricio's men, counting money. I motioned to Carlo, and he looked inside and pointed at two of our guys to take them out. They slid on facemasks and threw a smoke bomb inside. I grabbed two masks from Carlo's hands for Sabrina and myself. Carlo busted in the door and started shooting. Bodies kept dropping, but I stayed focused on keeping Sabrina safe and near me.

"I didn't expect you to get this far," Mauricio said,

holding his hands up as our men pulled him from the bathroom.

"You think hiding out would save you?"

"I had to do it; Joaquin was selling me out," Mauricio responded.

"So, talking to the DEA and trying to get me locked up was your out?" I questioned.

"'If Joaquin and the De Luca cartel were distracted with things crumbling around them, then I could get rid of Laurent and take over everything," Mauricio explained.

"You were never smart enough to be a don, Mauricio."

Bruno punched Mauricio in the face.

"What about my company?" Sabrina asked.

"Extra leverage to keep Antonio preoccupied if he knew his precious Bella might go to jail." Mauricio spat out the blood from his mouth, and it leaked down his chin.

"You son-of-a-bitch; I could have been destroyed!" Sabrina started to charge toward him.

He laughed. One of his men stopped her and grabbed her arm.

"Baby, I would never let that happen," I assured her.

"I have to say, you held your own against Agent Roberts," Mauricio goaded her.

Bruno kicked him in the stomach, and he screamed.

"Laurent can't save you now," I told him.

I gave Sabrina the gun, and she lifted it. I held onto her waist as she narrowed her eyes at him and shot him in the forehead.

"Let's go home," she said, turning to me and kissing my lips. I squeezed her waist and groaned as her hand gripped the nape of my neck.

Picturing her shooting that gun into Mauricio's head without even flinching brought out the animal in me once we got back to the house. I'd called my mother and told her to take the kids out with Emilia and stay gone for as long as possible. We'd had sex on and off for the last six hours, with only a few seconds to stop and eat—and that was me eating chocolate and strawberries off her stomach. I wanted to mark my name everywhere on her body.

I held her legs spread out at the corner of the pool and sucked on her engorged slick folds. Sabrina moaned and jerked forward as I held her both her thighs tight. Her face twisted in pleasure as I cupped her throbbing wet pussy. Her hand reached down and kept my head in place as she arched her back. "Yes. Right there." Her ragged breaths went in and out.

I increased my torture with long sensual licks and ran a hand across her nipples, tweaking each one gently. "Like this?" I asked.

She tried to close her legs around my head when I stuck

a finger in her sweet core, and her muscles clamped around my hand. "Baby!" she screamed, and I quickly covered her mouth with my lips to avoid waking up the kids. Sabrina's loud moans would wake up the entire block if we had neighbors.

I grabbed her around the waist and brought her into the water with her back against the jet streams and pushed myself in, taking her breath away. Sabrina's arms clenched around my neck as I thrusted, picking up the pace. I noticed her eyes closed, and I needed her attention focused on me. "Look at me."

She shook her head.

"Look at me, Bella."

"Tony... please," Sabrina groaned, sticking her nails into my arms as I ran a hand across her abdomen. Seeing the tiger-striped scars from giving birth to all four of my children gave me purpose. Sabrina was the strongest woman I knew. She prided herself on never showing that she was self-conscious about her figure after each birth. "Oh!" she cried out.

I released my hold, pulled out, and lifted her onto the side of the pool. I jumped out.

"What are you doing?" Sabrina asked, out of breath.

"Taking this to the guest house." I lifted her swiftly and walked through the yard to the guesthouse that they often let the kids use when friends came over. It had all the amenities of a one-bedroom apartment. I pushed the door open and carried her through the living room and down the hall to the bedroom. I planted her on the bed. My mouth covered hers as I centered my dick at her entrance and plunged inside.

"Ugh... baby," she panted as I circled my hips.

I smacked her hand down when she tried to push me away. "Take it." I thrusted harder, leaning my leg on the edge of the bed. I leaned my head back, closing my eyes and taking in her soft moans and grunts of pleasure. I felt the rise of my orgasm at its peak. I slid a hand around her neck and lightly squeezed.

Her heart-shaped lips opened slightly in a gasp. "Yes! Oh," Sabrina sighed, smiling in relief and gripping my upper arms. She brought me down on top of her and licked my bottom lip as our sweaty bodies came down from our high.

After a few seconds, I fell to the side of the bed and stared at the ceiling, thinking of the day we had with Mauricio.

"You okay?" I heard Sabrina's soft voice.

"Are you?" I turned to the side and propped my head on my elbow.

"I'm more worried about Isabella," she answered, running a finger across my chest and up to my cheek.

"We can talk with them tomorrow."

"She's my baby, Tony; what if something would have gone wrong?"

"Shush... don't think like that."

"Her screams and crying were too much."

"If I could kill him again, I would."

"Did they destroy the building?" Sabrina asked.

"I texted Carlo to burn it down."

"Let's get some sleep, and we can talk tomorrow," Sabrina said and curled up against me.

I nodded before lifting her palm and placing a kiss on it.

* * *

THE NEXT MORNING, I woke up in bed alone. I jumped up and showered in the guesthouse before coming into the main house to see the kids, Sabrina, and my mother, talking with Emilia. "You let me oversleep," I said, watching Sabrina feed Enzo fruit.

"I knew you needed your rest," Sabrina said.

I went to the counter and poured a cup of coffee, then took a sip. I stared at AJ, laughing with Jonathan over a video game.

"Pops, are you staying in today?" AJ asked.

I nodded, lifting my cup to take a sip. I picked up the remote, turned the volume up on the TV, and saw the news of Mauricio's death. The phone rang, and I grabbed it before one of the kids could.

"You see it?" Carlo asked.

I stole a piece of fruit off Enzo's plate. "Send a gift to the police and let Laurent know we'll be in touch soon." I ended the call and sat between Sabrina and Isabella. "Good morning, sweetheart." I pulled her into my lap.

"Morning, Daddy." Isabella continued to brush her doll's hair.

"I'm spending the day with you. What would you like to do?"

"Can we have tea time?" Isabella asked.

I groaned in aggravation at having to sit on the floor. I wasn't the same twentysomething guy anymore.

"Can you play video games with us first?" AJ questioned.

"After we have a talk."

"About what?" AJ wondered.

"Your mother and I want to see you in my office."

"I haven't gotten into trouble since I've been here," AJ argued and stomped out of the kitchen.

I moved Isabella back into her seat and went looking for AJ. I caught him by the elbow and pulled him into my office. "The attitude is done. Do you hear me?"

"Yeah," AJ mumbled, head down.

"I know I taught you to look a man in his eyes."

AJ glanced up at me.

"I'm not stupid, son; I know Bruno has been teaching you how to shoot."

His mouth opened and closed.

"Anything to say?" I asked.

"No."

"I didn't hear you correctly." I leaned over with my hand on my ear.

"No, *sir.*"

"Those boys you hang around with, Jarvis and Bobby, will no longer have any contact with you."

"That's not fair!" AJ fussed and plopped down in a chair.

"You only have yourself to blame for doing dumb shit."

He sucked his teeth.

"You are Antonio De Luca, Jr., and you will act like it." I pointed in his face.

"You act like *you're* an innocent angel!" AJ yelled.

"I don't need to act like anything other than the boss of all bosses. I'm the Don of the De Luca cartel."

"One day, I'll be the next boss; Uncle Bruno can teach me," he muttered.

I gripped him by his shirt, lifting him out of the chair.

"Antonio!" Sabrina shouted, storming into the office.

"Bella, he needs to learn."

"No, he needs his father." She stood next to him.

"I wouldn't be this hard on you if I didn't love you. I want you to be better than me," I said.

"He will be," Sabrina said, running a hand up my back.

I sighed, let him go, and sat on the edge of the desk. "If your grandfather was here now…" I chuckled. Looking at AJ was like staring in a mirror at myself; he had the same attitude and defiance that I gave to my father and brother growing up.

"I'm sorry," he said.

"If you want to learn how to shoot, I'll teach you. And no more Jarvis and Bobby."

"Yes, sir." He stood up, hugged his mother, and extended a hand for me to shake, then left the room.

"We have time," Sabrina said, leaning her back against my chest.

I wrapped my arms around her waist. "I want him homeschooled."

"He's going to fight us on that."

"I don't care; as we get bigger and make more enemies, I don't want to take a chance and leave myself open."

"All the kids?" Sabrina turned in my arms and kissed me, pulling at my bottom lip.

I grasped her ass. "Yeah, hire someone to teach them. I don't care about the cost."

"You're really staying in and hanging out with the kids?" Sabrina asked.

"Yep, and where are you going?"

"I'm having lunch with Liz and Janice."

"I'm not sure about that, Bella."

"Will it make you feel better if we have it here?" Sabrina asked.

"Yes, sweetheart."

"Okay, I'll tell them to come here." Sabrina lifted the phone and started to dial Janice's number. I stopped the call and sucked on the side of her neck. "Mmmm... you're not tired from last night?" Sabrina asked in a sultry voice.

"I'm avoiding going to spend tea time with our daughter," I said.

She laughed, pushing me away. I groaned and wiped the lipstick residue off my lips. I smacked her on the ass and went to eat before I got my day started. I went back into the kitchen to grab a plate of food. I sat down next to Enzo and Isabella as they laughed at cartoons on TV.

"Dad, are we living here for a while?" Jonathan asked.

"No, we'll be going back home in a few months."

"I think it's cool if we stay," Jonathan said.

"You know, your family tree is from here."

"Was it hard when you started dating Mom in the beginning?" Jonathan questioned.

"For her, not me. I fell in love with her the moment I met her."

"Daddy, I can't wait to fall in love," Isabella said.

I dropped my fork on my plate. "Pumpkin, you're not allowed to date until you're 50."

"Tony, don't tell her that," my mother said, picking up their plates to clean them.

"She needs to know the truth now, rather than later, when she tries to date."

"You're a De Luca for sure." Mom turned on the faucet and emptied the leftover food into the trash.

The house was full of kids, and the men were talking in Antonio's office. I expected to have a little girl-time to catch up over drinks and lunch, but Bruno and Carlo wanted to tag along, and that meant the kids wanted to come and see their cousins. I asked Maria and Emilia to help prepare enough food for everybody but told them to leave us alone. The husbands were babysitting. I had the gazebo next to the guesthouse set for us to be outside.

"The wine is so smooth," Janice commented, taking another sip of red wine.

"I needed a little girl-time after yesterday."

"What happened after we left?" Janice asked.

I picked up the fork and took a bite of baked potato. "I talked Antonio into taking me with them, and we killed Mauricio."

"I miss all the fun," Janice huffed, pouring dressing on her salad.

"When he held a gun to my daughter's face, I just wanted to rip his eyes out."

"I know how you feel," Liz said.

"Are you still staying here or coming back with us?" I asked.

"I told Bruno I wanted to stay here for now," Liz answered.

"How did things work out with James?" Janice questioned.

"Antonio told me that he got Senator Davis to fire him."

"How did that happen?" Liz inquired.

"From what he told me; his boss pulled rank on him for stalking us."

"Good, because he was trying a little too hard for somebody who was looking to help his friend," Janice explained.

"Him and his partner got fired."

"I heard he has a wife and kid," Janice said.

"I'm sorry that his wife has to be married to him."

"What about my baby, AJ? Is everything okay with him?" Janice queried, pouring more wine into her glass.

"Yeah, we had a long talk, and Antonio wants them to go back to homeschooling."

"I'll pray for you because my kids will stay in Grandberry," Janice joked, shaking her head.

"To think Mauricio could have taken me and my husband down."

"You've been 15 years strong, Sabrina; nothing can break you two," Liz said.

Janice took a gulp of her wine.

"That's true," I agreed. "But if he would have succeeded with getting me on some type of tax fraud..."

"You can't think like that," Liz told me.

"I know, but my family worked hard for our business."

"Have you talked to your parents about it yet?" Liz asked.

"I plan on calling them."

"Your dad will probably come back on if he thinks you need help," Janice said.

I agreed. "He would jump at the chance, but I want him to enjoy retirement."

"I liked your idea of bringing in a partner," Janice remarked.

I'd been thinking about it over the past few weeks, since this all started. "I would need someone who I could really trust and felt like family."

"Look at them, sitting over there, drinking and smoking cigars," Janice said.

I looked behind me at Carlo, Antonio, and Bruno, talking in the office. We could see them through the window. My husband gave me goosebumps every time I looked at him and saw that beautiful smile on his face that he rarely let anyone see.

"You look like you're ready to give him another baby," Janice teased.

I flipped her off. The baby shop was closed for me, and I would never open it again. "Never going to happen," I said.

"Never say never," Janice taunted, motioning her glass at me in a celebratory toast.

"No more wine for you," I said and removed the bottle from her side of the table.

We watched the kids come outside with my mother-in-law. Antonio, Carlo, and Bruno followed. They had their swim trunks on and towels ready to get in the pool. The kids got anything they wanted. The tough hardnose Antonio was weak for his kids. I laughed at Isabella, wagging her finger at Antonio; I assumed she was yelling about something. I noticed him grab her hair cover, which he probably forgot.

"He's learning," I said.

"Have you guys ever dreamed about being married to somebody else?" Liz asked.

"What do you mean?" Janice inquired, taking a cupcake off the dessert table in the corner.

"Think about it: If we never would have given them a second look, would our lives still have crossed paths?" Liz asked, shrugging and biting into her sandwich.

"I had a dream once that I never met Antonio and never had kids," I said.

"How did it feel?" Janice poured more wine into her glass.

"It felt like I was in an alternate universe or something." I laughed, shaking my head at the thought.

"Well, who was the guy?" Janice asked.

"You'll curse me out if I say it."

"Don't tell me—Alex?" she questioned.

"Yep. Basically, he never cheated, and we got married, but somehow I was still miserable."

"That should tell you something," Janice remarked.

"What?"

"Even staying with Alex, your life would have been boring, safe, and uncomplicated. You need fire, passion, and devotion," Janice reminded me.

I looked over at Antonio, helping Isabella into the pool. "Never a dull moment with Antonio."

"We need to have more lunches together. I miss my girls," Janice announced, holding up her glass for a toast.

"I agree. And next time, we'll invite Sofia and Cassidy," I agreed and took a sip of my wine.

We continued to catch up and talk about our families, and the next vacation spot we could all go to.

ANTONIO

*O*ne Month Earlier

I was working in my office, watching a video that the senator sent to me of Agent Roberts, talking to his supervisor. I turned the volume up and listened while he argued about me being corrupt:

"How much did he pay you off for?"

"Roberts, I suggest you get your head out of your ass," Special-Agent-in-Charge Miguel Sheen said.

"I know you're on his payroll," Roberts told him.

"James, you tried and failed.."

"Because you let him win!" James yelled, pacing back and forth in front of his desk.

"When was the last time you took a vacation?" Miguel asked.

"Harry was right about you," James said.

"Harry only cares about making it to his retirement pension. I suggest you try to do the same."

"I refuse to give up. I can still get his wife on something."

"The business is clean, James; it's over."

"No! I need more time," James said.

"I'm not letting you waste money on a case you can't win," Miguel said.

"A case that I was *this close* to solving and bringing down Antonio de Luca, the notorious mobster."

"Where's the witnesses? What about the evidence on Camilla and Derrick?" Miguel countered and stood.

"He covered up for her. Don't you get it?! That asshole will do anything to make sure she's seen as the perfect little wife," James spat.

"What are you watching?" Sabrina questioned.

I muted the sound. "James getting fired."

"Where did you get this video from?" Sabrina asked, coming around my desk to sit in my lap.

"Davis sent it to me as confirmation."

"You think it's finally over?" Sabrina wondered, picking up the file on James Roberts.

"It won't be over unless I'm dead," I said.

"Don't talk like that."

"Have I told you how much I love you?" I asked.

"You tell me all the time," Sabrina said, playing with my tie.

"Harry could have been paid off, but James was obsessed with us."

"I think that's an understatement."

I tightened my hold on her waist and turned the volume back up:

"I can't approve of what you've done. I don't think it's how the agency works," Miguel explained.

"I've given my life to this agency, and this is how you repay me?" he hissed, tossing everything on the desk to the floor.

"All you had to do was play nice," Miguel replied.

"You're in his pockets, just like the rest of them."

"No, I'm thinking about my family and job," Miguel told him and handed him some papers.

James slowly removed his badge and gun and placed them on the desk. He yanked the papers out of Miguel's hand and stormed out of the room.

That was the same time he busted into Sabrina's office, and she called me, saying he was talking crazy to her.

"How about you come to bed, and I show you my appreciation?" Sabrina whispered and nibbled on my ear.

"I'd like that, Mrs. De Luca."

* * *

Present Day

The day had been long, full of hanging out, eating, swimming with the kids, and playing video games that Jonathan beat me at until I finally gave up before deciding to throw it in the trash.

I grunted at the phone ringing in the middle of the night, disturbing Bella from her sleep. I hurried to answer, and I pulled her closer in my arms with her back to my chest.

My phone rang. "hello?" I groggily answered.

Sabrina scooted her ass closer against my dick. We'd just gone to sleep two hours ago, after making love.

"We have them," Salvatore said.

I heard crying on the other end of the phone. "Am I on speaker phone?"

"Yes, sir."

"Jarvis and Bobby, it's Mr. De Luca," I said.

Salvatore and some of my men had gone to Jarvis's house to scare the boys and make it clear that if they got my son caught up in more shit, I would make an example out of them.

"Please, don't kill me! Please!" Jarvis screamed.

I blew out a breath in annoyance. "Shush… no one is going to kill you."

"Who is that?" I heard another voice.

"If you don't know who I am, then I think you should be grateful," I replied.

"That's Antonio De Luca," Bobby mumbled.

"No need for an introduction, Bobby," I replied. "I'm going to make this quick."

"Please, let us go," Jarvis cried somberly.

"Moving forward, you will no longer have any contact with AJ," I replied. "Do I make myself clear."

"Yes, sir," they both said.

"Good, and if you see him walking down the street, then go in the opposite direction. If I hear you've defied me, then you'll see if all the rumors are true."

I ended the call and buried my face in Sabrina's neck. I slid one arm across her stomach, pulling her tighter to snuggle.

"Who was that?" she asked, cupping my cheek.

"Nobody. Go back to sleep, Bella." I kissed the inside of her palm and fell back to sleep.

* * *

SABRINA WANTED to have more family time while we were in Italy, and I promised to cut down on my meetings and relax a little more. The next afternoon, we packed the kids up and headed to my yacht. The car stopped at the dock, and I helped Isabella and Enzo get out. My mother carried their bags of toys. I helped Sabrina get out. She was wearing a one-piece bathing suit underneath a white see-through dress that she had to fight me to wear. My wife was getting sexier day by day.

"This is beautiful, baby," Sabrina said, putting her hand on my lower back as we walked up the dock and onto the boat.

The captain shook hands with me and AJ. I saw my mother looking out at the water, and the birds flying overhead as Enzo giggled and laughed. The yacht was worth over $2 million, and I had it built a few years ago after Jonathan was born. It had 12 rooms, including a master suite, a large swimming pool and Jacuzzi area, a movie theatre, a spa, an outdoor fireplace, and a wintergarden deck. Once, Sabrina asked if we could travel around the world if I ever retired, but I doubted that my life would ever be free from being the Don.

The crew assisted everyone onboard, and I watched as AJ and Jonathan stepped onboard. "Baby, go ahead and let me talk to AJ really quick." I passed Enzo over to her and put Isabella down to walk on her own. "You good?" I asked AJ.

"Yeah. Why?" AJ responded.

"I'm just checking to make sure you're okay."

"Mom told me about doing homeschooling again," he sighed, sliding his hands into his pockets. He squared his shoulders and made eye contact with me.

"You know why I'm so hard on you?"

"No."

"Because you scare me."

"What?!"

"You're just like me, AJ. In every way. If I were like my father, I wouldn't care about you, and I'd push you toward taking over the business. But I see better things for you."

"Dad."

"No, I want you to be better; if not for me and your mother, then for yourself."

"I hear you." He kicked a rock into the water.

I stretched my arm around his neck and walked up the deck onto the boat. "Besides, when you try to start dating, you are going to need me."

"Why do you say that?" he asked.

"Have you met Sabrina De Luca?" I joked

He burst into laughter. "Mom can be pretty dramatic," AJ replied.

I narrowed my eyes at his statement. "That's your mother, AJ. Only I can call her dramatic."

"Sure, padre," he said.

"Let's go relax."

"I tried calling Bobby back home, but his mom said he was living with his Dad now. Then I tried calling Jarvis and got no answer." AJ pulled out his phone, showing me the call log.

"That's strange," I responded.

I brought him in close and kissed the top of his head as we walked over to my mother and Enzo, still watching the birds fly. I'd never admit to him that every decision I made was in his best interest, like keeping bad influences like Jarvis and Bobby away from him before they got older and understood the power that AJ would have if he chose this life.

"Uncle Bruno!" AJ screamed when my brother came up behind him and picked him up.

"How's my favorite nephew?" Bruno asked.

"Good," AJ replied.

Bruno let him go, ruffling his hair. Already, my first-born was standing at 5'7" at 14 years old. I could only imagine how tall he'd be when he reached 18.

"AJ, let me talk to your uncle for a second," I said.

AJ shoved his uncle playfully in the shoulder and ran off.

"What's up, little brother?" Bruno asked.

"Showing him how to shoot a gun?"

"He needs to know," Bruno replied, folding his arms.

"Then I will show him. I'm not raising him like our father raised us."

"Is this you being angry or Sabrina?" he questioned.

I glared at him. "I will forget you brought my wife into this discussion."

"You and I both know he's going to be the next in line as the boss of the family," Bruno explained.

"He can make that choice when he's older, not now. You remember how it was, going out at night to bury the bodies of our enemies. We were both too young."

"He's a good shot," Bruno responded.

"That's not the point."

"AJ has darkness in him," Bruno said. "We can't hide this life from him." He tapped me on the shoulder and pointed at AJ, who was talking to Jonathan.

I sighed, slid my hand into my pockets, and looked at what the future held.

ANTONIO

wo Months Later
The kids had kept us busy today, after we picked them up from school. I hadn't had a minute to be alone with my wife since we got back from Italy two months ago. Every other day, it was something new; someone either wanted to show me something or ask for something that only I could provide. I was lucky to have a patient wife who understood the way our business worked, and when I needed time away, it wasn't because of anything that could bring up rumors of infidelity. We'd worked past that years ago, and trust was our most honored gift between us.

I wrapped my hand around my whiskey glass, stood against the dresser, and watched Sabrina undress in front of me.

"You plan on standing there all day?" Sabrina asked, stepping out of her dress and kicking it to the side. Her long legs were accentuated by her heels; something about her calf muscles turned me on when she was in this mood.

My hard shaft pulsed in my pants. She walked toward

me and pressed her body against my chest. She took the glass out of my hand and gulped the rest down. She placed the empty glass on top of the table and leaned in to kiss my lips.

My hands found themselves sliding down her body, feeling her bare hips, ass, and breasts. I leaned down to take her breast in my mouth, teasing and sucking at her taut dark nipple. My other hand parted her pussy from the back, feeling her flowing juices. "Hmmm... mmm. I want you on your knees," I said, releasing her breasts.

"Oh... oh," she purred, switching over to the bed and training her eyes on me.

I licked my lips and removed my shirt and pants, while she squirmed on the bed, playing with herself. I grabbed the bottle of whiskey and poured some of it down my throat. I stalked to the bed and captured the sexiest mouth I'd ever seen, sucking on her bottom lip. I trailed a hand up her legs, across her skin. I pecked her lips and nipped at her skin, then soothed it with my tongue.

"Please... fuck me." Sabrina whispered, cupping both sides of my face and pushing her tongue into my mouth.

I moved to cover her body with mine and pushed her legs back to her shoulders, pressing the head of my dick to her tight asshole and pushed forward as she tensed. I stopped, letting her get acclimated again. "Shit!" I said, thrusting slowly as my sweat beads fell onto her stomach. I quickly pulled out and flipped her onto her stomach.

She arched her back, and I slapped her ass. She pushed back into me, trying to control my movements, and I slapped both her ass cheeks again. "Yes!" Sabrina shouted, gripping the sheets.

"Who are you?" I questioned.

"Sabrina De Luca!"

"Show me." I pulled out, and she turned around, gripping my erection and sliding her tongue across the tip. She stared up into my eyes as she pleased me, while fondling my balls. "You're sexy as fuck, baby."

She moaned, taking in a deep breath and sliding me farther down her throat. Then she released me and took in a sharp breath as I pushed her back onto the bed and rode the wave of her warm wet pussy to the brink. "Ahhh... I'm coming!" Sabrina cried out.

I thrusted faster, feeling her pleasure cover my dick. I was right behind her as my orgasm traveled up my body, and I filled her with more of my babies.

I fell to the side of the bed, out of breath. Sabrina inched closer and wrapped her arm around my waist. Her right leg lay across my stomach. I kissed her forehead. Seeing her at the meeting, speaking as the Donna of the family, was such a turn-on that I was afraid she could lead the family better than me.

"What are you thinking about?" she asked, maneuvering her hair from under my arm. I gripped her thigh, angling her entire body on top of me. She rested her elbow on my chest, cupping her chin in her palm.

"You."

"What *about* me?"

"I've loved you for so long; I can't imagine anyone else as my wife."

"Is that right?"

"Yes, Bella. I know in the beginning; I was a hothead."

"Please, you're *still* a hothead. You remember that time you busted into my office and called me a bitch?" She sucked her teeth.

"I apologized for that."

She tried to move off me, and I placed both hands on her waist to keep her from moving. "You wouldn't want AJ acting like an ass to get a girl," she argued.

"I pray AJ finds someone who's like his mother: a beautiful, smart, and headstrong woman."

"Good answer."

"Honestly, you took my breath away, and I was still trying to figure out if I could bring you into my world."

"You never seemed nervous or regretted our relationship."

"I'll never regret loving you. I was more scared of my world changing *you*."

"It has, but it wasn't all bad, getting to wake up next to you and our children," Sabrina said, tracing her index finger along my forehead, cheek, and chin.

"Even through the dangerous parts, you've stepped up and made decisions to protect this family, and I admire you," I said. "No matter what the other bosses say."

"Being a bitch comes in handy sometimes," she joked.

A knock at the door caused me to pull up the blankets to cover us. "Who is it?" I asked.

"Daddy, I want to sleep with you and Mommy," Isabella said.

Sabrina rolled her eyes.

I chuckled and kissed her lips. I jumped up, picked up my boxers, and slid my robe on before I opened the door. Isabella was in her Supergirl pajamas, and her hair was all over her head. She was rubbing her sleepy eyes. "What's wrong, pumpkin?" I asked.

I let her walk inside, and she went to the bed, climbing in next to her mother. "I had a bad dream," Isabella said.

"What was the dream about?" I questioned.

Sabrina waved her hand behind Isabella's back for me not to start. Everybody in the family knew that once Isabella started talking, they'd never get any rest.

"That you went away again," Isabella responded.

"Baby, you'll never have to worry about that," I told her.

Sabrina stepped out of bed with the sheet covering her body.

"What about Mommy?" Isabella asked.

"Honey, I'm never going away; you don't have to worry about us," Sabrina mentioned, heading back to bed to pick Isabella up and put her in her lap.

"Can we watch TV?" Isabella asked.

"Yes," I replied.

"No," Sabrina answered at the same time. Sabrina grimaced and popped me on the back of the head. I gave in to Isabella every time, and she was the only woman apart from my wife that I would put on a pedestal.

"What's wrong, Daddy?"

I rubbed the sting out and smirked at Sabrina. "Nothing, pumpkin. Let me take you back to your bed; Mommy had a bad dream, too, and she needs my help," I teased and picked Isabella up in my arms.

"Really? Mommy can watch movies with us. That always helps me fall asleep," Isabella said.

"I don't think Mommy wants to watch movies," I joked as the door slammed behind me. I kissed the top of Isabella's head and went to her bedroom. I stayed with her for the rest of the night, after reading her two bedtime stories.

* * *

TWO DAYS LATER, the family was having dinner at Antonio's together, along with our friends and their kids. Bruno made sure to close down the restaurant for us when I told him we hadn't been together in a while. Sabrina and I both dressed in dark blue, and her cocktail dress was form-fitting and short. I was thinking about stealing her away for a few minutes and taking her back to my office.

"Janice, have you decided what you're doing for your anniversary?" Sabrina asked.

The waitress brought out a bottle of red wine and poured some for all the ladies. I had scotch. AJ and the kids had soda, which we rarely let them have when they were at home. Emilia even came out to enjoy our little reunion.

"No, but Carlo needs to get his mind right if he wants to have another year as my husband," Janice blurted out, taking a sip of her wine.

"Baby, not now," Carlo said, trying to grab her hand.

She jerked back and pointed her finger in his face. "Don't get sweet with me now, Carlo. You know what you did," Janice stated, as the waiters brought our meals out.

"What did my brother do this time, Janice?" I asked, laughing at her hard glare.

"I forgot to take her out on a date because I was helping you," Carlo commented, and I thought of the last time we were together.

"Not just any date. We haven't had alone-time because of *your* three brats," Janice spat back at him.

"Mom!" all three of her kids groaned at their mother. Everybody knew how direct Janice was, and she never sugarcoated anything. Sabrina told me that she'd had the sex talk with them by having a sex education class in their garage with whiteboards and charts.

"Hush. How do you think you got here?" Janice asked, cutting into her steak.

"No more wine for you," Carlo said, moving her glass away from her. Everyone at the table laughed as Janice bit her bottom lip and pouted, folding her arms.

"Leave my best friend alone, Carlo," Sabrina said.

"Can you guys believe we're all married with kids now?" Liz shared, wiping her youngest son's mouth off.

"I can," Sabrina replied and covered her face with her palm on top of the table.

"AJ, you're getting so big, looking just like your father," Janice teased, pinching his cheeks. "I can see him now, breaking some little girl's heart."

"Auntie, stop." AJ blushed.

"What? You have that De Luca swag and attitude. A mixture of Antonio and Carlo," Janice responded.

"Same as CJ," I said.

My nephew grinned; he looked exactly like Carlo, and I suspected that Janice kept them on a tight leash.

"Do you need anything else, sir?" the waitress asked me, and I waved her off.

"You can stop flirting with my best friend's husband in our faces, maybe," Janice snapped, and Sabrina giggled.

"Excuse me," the waitress said. She was new and didn't know the dos and don'ts of how things ran around here when it came to our wives.

"Ignore her," Carlo explained, jumping up and reaching over to pull Janice out of her seat.

"I'm not finished eating," Janice said and grabbed the bottle of wine before they strolled away; I assumed to our office.

"We can't take those two anywhere," CJ mumbled, and the entire table burst into laughter.

"You know your parents best, nephew," I said.

The rest of the night was full of laughter and catching up with the kids about school and their friends. AJ and CJ wanted to go back to private school, and I was still not too fond of that big of a leap. But they were getting older, and I prided myself on being a better father and letting them have more opinions about their lives than I had growing up.

SABRINA

*O*ne Week Later

I opened the door of the conference room and strolled inside. My team was sitting around, talking and wondering what the meeting was about. After we had the DEA come in and try to shut us down behind my husband's back, I wanted to restructure, so my family's business didn't end up in another media storm.

"Thank you again for coming in early," I said, unbuttoning my jacket and sitting at the head of the table. My eyes scanned the room and saw Janice step inside and take the seat across from me.

"What's this about, Sabrina?" Gary asked.

"Gary, I wanted to have the heads of every department come in today. I'll be making an announcement," I replied.

"Is everything okay?" Josie, our accounting manager, inquired.

"Yes, everything is fine."

"Please, tell me the DEA isn't doing another investigation," Gary stated.

"No, Gary. You don't have to worry about that. I know

you're wondering about your job and worried about having money for your 1-900 number dates," Janice commented.

I groaned. The both of them always went back and forth like two pitbulls, fighting for dominance.

"Aren't you Vice President?" Gary asked, jumping out of his seat.

"Yeah, so?" Janice answered, standing up.

I clapped my hands to get everybody's attention. "We are not doing this today. Janice, sit down—and you, too, Gary."

"Fine. But she needs to apologize," Gary said.

I looked at Janice, pleading with my eyes.

She blew out a breath in frustration. "I apologize, Gary; I didn't know it was a sensitive subject for you," Janice remarked, and the entire room erupted in laughter.

"See, this is the problem," Gary said, sitting back down.

"All right, you two, hush," I said. "Today, I'm moving Washington Finance into a trust and bringing in another partner."

"What?!" Josie shouted. The chatter grew louder in the room.

"This way, I can still make sure the business is safe from any interruptions," I explained. "My husband approached me with an offer that I couldn't pass up."

"Your husband who went to jail?" Gary asked.

"My husband was falsely brought up on charges."

"Who is this partner?" Josie asked.

"You already know them."

Janice rose from her seat.

"You have got to be kidding me." Gary grimaced and gave me a harsh stare.

"No, I'm not. She's already VP, and this is the next step. I want to continue spending more time with my family, and I know she'll continue to have the best interests of my family's business at heart," I said.

Everyone started talking at once.

"This is happening," I said. "So, either get onboard, or you can leave now."

Josie, Kerry, and the other board members nodded.

"Great," I replied. "So, I'll have the papers sent over today."

All the board members walked out of the conference room, except Janice and me.

"What do you think?" Janice asked.

"I think I made the right decision for our family."

"You think it's too early to let them know Liz is taking over my position as VP?" Janice questioned, as she picked up her file-folder.

I laughed at her question. "It might be, but at this point, I'm the Donna of the De Luca cartel. Either they get onboard, or I make them," I answered and winked.

She chuckled and hugged me. "How about we end the night with some drinks at Ryde tonight, where it all started?" Janice asked.

"Let's hope we don't end up with anymore mobsters falling into our laps," I joked and connected my arm with hers as we walked out of the conference room, laughing.

EPILOGUE, PART I: SABRINA

Six Months Later

Ryde had been expanded a few months ago, and Antonio knocked out the wall of the building next door. We were having our anniversary party there, and things were going well. The food smelled good, and all our friends came out to help us celebrate. The decorations were my favorite colors—baby blue and cream. H.E.R played throughout the club, as some of our friends and family started to drop off gifts.

Antonio knew how much I would have been happy with just me, him, and the kids, staying home and celebrating together, looking through photos of all our family vacations, and the kids' special events. But this was all I ever wanted in life—to have my family together as one.

I even got away with not hearing Antonio's mouth about my outfit. I'd picked out a cute pink one-shoulder cocktail dress with stiletto heels and minimal jewelry, since the dress enhanced my full breasts and neckline that Antonio loved to suck on every minute.

I waved at our parents as they started to walk toward

me with Isabella and Luca in their arms. Antonio took Luca out of my mom's arms and kissed his cheek. They both grinned at each other.

Janice was already up dancing, and Carlo was trying to keep her under control, but we all knew there was no way to control Janice. I giggled at her, running away from him every time he tried to stand behind her when she thought she could get away with twerking.

"I can't believe Janice is acting like a fool at her age." I laughed, pointing at her as she tried to hide behind Dimitri.

"You know, Janice is a special one," Mom's lips turned up in a smile, and she crossed her arms over her chest.

"How are you feeling?" Dad asked. "Almost 16 years together and still standing."

I turned to grab Isabella's cheek as she playfully hugged her grandpa around his neck. "I feel good, and I'm happy. Are you happy, Antonio?"

Antonio wrapped his arms around my shoulders and pulled me close. He whispered in my ear, "I can't wait to get you home in bed." He kissed the side of my forehead.

"Daddy, I want to go dance with Auntie Janice," Isabella said.

"Bella, you stay where I can see you," Antonio said.

My parents walked off with Luca and Isabella to the dance floor, and AJ was with his friends, trying to show Carlo the latest dance moves and impress some of the other family friends. I prayed every night that he wouldn't follow in his father's footsteps. The many fights that Antonio and I have had constantly dealt with AJ, and the idea of him growing up in a world that knows violence as the only solution.

Antonio frowned at Isabella, who was mimicking Janice, dancing behind Carlo.

I gripped his chin and pulled his focus back to me. "Stop frowning."

"She's growing up too fast," Antonio said.

"You're getting old," I replied.

He tried to pull away from my hand. "I can promise there's nothing old about me, Bella," Antonio teased, gripping me around the waist and leaning down to press a kiss on my lips.

"Mmmm… I can attest to you not being old, baby," I responded, pulling back and staring into his eyes.

"16 years, and these are the best days of my life."

"I want you to know nothing will ever keep us apart," I said.

"Good, because I'd hate to hurt somebody over you," Antonio remarked, looking down at my dress, holding my hands out, and smirking.

"Come on, let's have some champagne and get a dance in before you rip this dress off and have your way with me."

He licked his lips and led me to our group of friends, who were standing around, laughing and joking together. This was our family: the good, bad, and ugly of it all. And I was grateful that a man with all his faults and all the drama that came with being the head of a cartel could still be my hero, and the love of my life.

EPILOGUE, PART II: ANTONIO

One Year Later

The car stopped in front of my office building, and I jumped out, tugging on the cuffs of my jacket. I headed inside with Carlo and Joaquin behind me. We'd gotten word that Laurent Carrington was retiring and wanted to have a meeting before he made things official. The other bosses wanted to have a meeting about things, too, since Mauricio was no longer a factor in his business.

Dimitri opened my office door. I stepped inside and saw Laurent, sitting in a chair in front of my desk. I extended a hand and he reached out and shook it.

"Good to see you again, Laurent."

"You, too, Antonio. Carlo and Joaquin, I wasn't expecting you two to be here," Laurent commented.

I motioned for him to take a seat. "Anytime I have to handle business, I have my right hand with me."

"I understand, but I need to know I can have confidence in this conversation."

"Laurent, we've known each other for a long time."

"Laurent, what's this really about?" Carlo questioned, standing against the door next to Joaquin.

"I wasn't onboard with the killing of Mauricio, and now with me retiring, I have to know that the Carrington share will be upheld," Laurent announced.

I raised my eyebrows at his statement.

"Mauricio was stealing from you, Laurent; you should be thanking us," Joaquin said.

"Once I retire, I need to know that my family won't have any problems from the De Luca and Fuertes cartels," Laurent stated, standing.

"I can speak for both families who are making money together, so nothing will change—unless you do something that causes me to rethink this venture," I said.

"My daughter," he responded.

"What about your daughter?" I asked.

"She's going to take over and be the boss of the Carrington cartel," Laurent mentioned and hurried out of my office.

I didn't have a problem with a woman running a drug cartel, but I knew his daughter wasn't for this life. The last time we saw her at Joaquin's party, she was more interested in running away from it.

"What are you thinking?" Carlo questioned, coming forward to sit on the edge of my desk.

"I think Laurent is setting himself up for a fight when the other bosses hear about this change," I replied, sitting back in my seat and stared at the ceiling thoughtfully.

"The Carrington cartel is always unpredictable," Joaquin said.

"Says the guy from the Fuertes cartel," I joked.

"The De Luca cartel is just as crazy," Carlo said.

"To think this all started with my father. Now, I'm the

boss of all bosses," I remarked, thinking of my journey to this position.

"The next generation," Carlo said, pulling his ringing phone out of his pocket.

"AJ is already itching to be involved."

"Then teach him better than your father taught you," Joaquin explained.

"I just hope he doesn't have a monster inside of him and become like me."

"The cartel lifestyle calls for a little bit of a monster," Carlo said.

"I just hope Sabrina's ready."

My son was already asking questions and wanting me to take him to the gun range more and more. I needed to keep an extra eye on him when he was around his friends, and if AJ wanted to be in the business, then I'd have to deal with his mother—and that fight would be a never-ending story.

* * *

I hope you enjoyed Antonio and Sabrina's story. If you want more "Mafia Romance, why not try *Joaquin Fuertes* here* https://books2read.com/u/mvZlgV

Have you read *"Temptation yet?* That is a standalone contemporary, sports, curvy girl romance.

Please also check out my Heart of Stone Series" https://books2read.com/u/boWPAV

Please also check out my **Mutual Agreement** " https://books2read.com/u/mgzzWX a steamy political romance.

Have you checked out **"She's All I Need"** click here https://books2read.com/u/49lkeW a sports, opposites attract romance.

"Heart of Stone Book 4" here https://books2read.com/u/4NXyPG with a host of characters intertwined.

If you love billionaire romance check out **"Heart of Stone 1" here** https://books2read.com/u/boWPAV with a host of characters intertwined.

SNEAK PEEK: THE CARRINGTON CARTEL

Gigi's future has always been known. She's to marry into the Ramini family. To her family, nothing matters more than that.

As the daughter of the renowned Laurent Carrington, long-time gunrunner and drug trafficker for the cartel, nothing about Gigi's life is ambiguous. She does what her father says—or suffers the consequences.

Axel is good at his job. As lead enforcer for a notorious cartel associate, he's entrusted to monitor Gigi's every move. What he doesn't expect is to fall in love with her. Now, he's faced with a tough choice—one that could cost him his life if he's not careful.

Will Gigi's plan to keep her arranged marriage at bay shield her from her father's wrath? Or will her budding relationship with Axel lead her down an ugly path?

ORDER OF STRUCK OF LOVE UNIVERSE

Order of Reading
　　The Early Years-A Prequel Short Story
https://books2read.com/u/49Zjnw
Ruthless Struck In Love Book 1
https://books2read.com/u/4AxKLo
Savage Struck In Love Book 2
https://books2read.com/u/bpED6g
Beast Struck In Love Book 3
https://books2read.com/u/3LpgdJ
Janice and Carlo Captivated By His Love
https://books2read.com/u/b6je6M
Brutal Struck In Love Book 4
https://books2read.com/u/4NQyE9
Stolen-Fuertes Mafia Cartel Book 1
https://books2read.com/u/mvZlgV
Saved-Fuertes Mafia Cartel Book 2
https://books2read.com/u/4DWwLd
Redemption Struck In Love Book 5
https://books2read.com/u/b5kZ8O

Betrayal- Fuertes Mafia Cartel Book 3
https://books2read.com/u/4A5LGp

ORDER OF SERIES HEART OF STONE

Heart of Stone Book 1 Emery and Jackson
https://books2read.com/u/boWPAV
Heart of Stone Book 1.5
https://payhip.com/b/kWg7
Heart of Stone Book 2 Jordan and Damon
https://books2read.com/u/ba2OMx
Heart of Stone Book 3.5 Bottoms Up
https://payhip.com/b/HGP1
Heart of Stone Book 3 Angela and Brent
https://books2read.com/u/31rx9l
Heart of Stone Book 4 Jessica and Joseph
https://books2read.com/u/4NXyPG

CATALOG RELEASES

The Early Years-A Prequel Short Story

Struck in Love 1, 2, 3,4,5

Heart of Stone, Book 1 (Emery & Jackson)

Heart Of Stone Book 1.5 Emery &Jackson A Valentine's Day Short

Janice and Carlo: Captivated By His Love

Heart of Stone, Book 2 (Jordan and Damon)

Temptation

Heart of Stone, Book 3 (Angela and Brent)

Bottoms Up Heart of Stone, Book 3.5(Jessica and Joseph Short

Cocky Catcher

Bossy Billionaire

Love Shorts:A Collection of Short Stories

Stolen Fuertes Mafia Cartel Book 1

Saved Fuertes Mafia Cartel Book 2

Exposed (Salvation Society Novel)

Betrayal Fuertes Mafia Cartel Book 3

Refuel(A Driven World Novel)

Pressure(A Driven World Novel)

Until Serena(HEA World Novel)
Exposed (Salvation Society Novel)
Heart of Stone, Book 4 (Jessica and Joseph)
She's All I Need
Something Gaine(Romantic Comedy)

304 PUBLISHING COMPANY

We showcase authors who write African-American, interracial, women's fiction, urban romance, erotic, and contemporary romance novels, along with thriller, suspense, poetry, beauty, and style books.

Thank you for taking the time to visit us. Join our mailing list to stay updated with new releases and blog posts.

"Antonio and Sabrina Struck In Love Series"
1. Heather Headley- In My Mind
2. Love on the Brain -Rihanna
3. Cockiness -Rihanna
4. 7/11- Beyonce
5. Crazy In Love- Beyonce
6. Radioactive- Imagine Dragons
7. When We- Tank
8. Insecure- Jasmine Sullivan
9. Ain't Too Proud to Beg- The Temptations
10. You Keep Me Hanging On-The Supremes
11. Be Without You- Mary J Blige
12. Fire and Desire- Rick James & Teena Marie
13. I'd Rather Go Blind- Etta James
14. Make You Feel My Love- Adele
15. Lost Without U- Robin Thicke
16. Apologize- One Republic

AUTHOR BIO

Chiquita Dennie is an Author, Award winning Filmmaker and Podcast Host. Her first short film "Invisible" released in Summer 2017 and screened in multiple festivals and won for Best Short Film. Also, hosts a podcast that showcases the latest in Beauty, Business and Community called "Moscato and Tea." Her debut release of Antonio and Sabrina Struck In Love has opened a new avenue of writing that she loves.

Chiquita lives in Los Angeles, CA. Before she started writing contemporary romance, worked in the entertainment Industry on notable TV shows Dr Phil show, Tyra Banks show, American Idol, and Deal or No Deal. But her favorite job is the one she's now doing full time writing romance.

If you want to know when the next book will come out, please visit my website at http://www.304publishing.com, where you can sign up to receive an email for my next release.

WHAT'S NEXT?!

Want to know what happens next?

Struck in Love 3 is available on Amazon now.

Reviews are the lifeblood of the publishing world. They're read, appreciated, and needed. Please consider taking the time to leave a few words on Amazon.

Sign up for updates and sneak peeks at the site below. www.chiquitadennie.com